IT'S KIND OF A BUNNY STORY

Hey There, Hop Stuff Book 3

Sedona Ashe

Cover artwork by Sanja Gombar

https://bookcoverforyou.com/

Interior Design & Formatting by Inessa Sage

https://www.cauldronpress.ca/

A huge thank you to-

Allison Woerner for Alpha Reading.

Maxine Meyer for Copy Editing.

Emily LeVault for Proofreading & Editing.

Meg Kelly for being an amazing assistant!

I want to thank my readers from the bottom of my heart for rallying around me the past several months while I focused on my health. There were so many days where I was frustrated or struggling, but I'd see a message or comment from one of you guys and it would turn my day around. I think every author is terrified to take a break from writing for fear their readers will forget about them or their characters. But not only did my readers show me through those comments and messages that they're not going anywhere, their love and understanding helped to remind me of how much I love telling and sharing stories. I always hope that my books will make someone laugh when they're having a rough day, or help them escape when life sucks. Thank you for doing the same for me these past months when I needed a bit of sunshine in my life.

All my love,

Sedona

It's kind of a Bunny Story

3

Hey There, Hop Stuff

SEDONA ASHE

CONTENTS

Sensitivity Note

It's Kind of a Bunny Story starts with a bang… well, more like a lot of *banging.* So, if you like your novels hot enough to compete at a pepper eating contest, I think you're going to love this book! If the only spice you enjoy is salt (or you don't triple the amount of garlic a recipe calls for because you know it'll be bland otherwise), then you might want to skim read the first few chapters and jump straight into the twist-filled story!

Charlee has gone through a lot in her past, so there are mentions of what she's experienced. For example, the women in her burrow are treated as pets and given little choice in who they are shared with. While that is discussed, all steamy scenes in this book are fully consensual! There is mention of violence in her past, as well as some violence when she faces those in the burrow again.

Chapter ONE

CHARLEE

"Charlee? Are you here?" Fletcher's words were followed by a huffed laugh through the tunnel as he made his way toward me. "Of course you are. I can smell you."

"Are you saying I stink?" I tried to hiss, only to cringe at my voice's unfamiliar breathiness.

This dang heat made me sound as though I was moments away from singing the happy birthday song for a president. Maybe this was a good time to consider a career with a phone sex company. I'd make a killing with my new voice—as long as I kept from bursting out laughing at the ridiculous things the desperate men moaned into the phone.

A sharp cramp attempted to contort my insides into a pretzel, reminding me that I wouldn't likely need a job since I would be taking an early retirement from life within a few days. You didn't have to worry about mortgage payments and grocery bills when you were tucked away in a quiet cemetery.

My death was entirely preventable—if I'd bowed to the will of my burrow. But I'd rather die on my own terms than have my body used as a personal toy by the arrogant cottonhole males that ran my burrow.

The only thing more unfair than being passed around like a trading card without a say in who would share my bed, was that my inner rabbit would bond to whatever random males bred me during my first heat. Why should I have had to pine after and long for males who'd probably won the right to my virgin heat in a drunken poker game? Males who'd take part in breeding every other female in the burrow.

A soft glow came from the dark tunnel that led out of the cave, and moments later, Fletcher appeared, a glowing orb in one hand and a pile of blankets and pillows in his arms. "Cillian, the alpha of the pack, gave me this light. Apparently, they float in pools to give ambience to parties," Fletcher explained as I stared at the light he'd sat on a rock ledge near me.

"Huh. Technology is something else," I commented as I admired the amber light it cast on the stone walls. The cave was about as far from glamping as you could get, but I appreciated the cozy lighting.

Fletcher kneeled beside me, pulling me against his chest. "And for the record, you never stink—except for that one time you fell in the compost heap."

Burying his nose in my hair, he took a deep breath. He did his best to hide it, but I caught the way his breath hitched, and his body trembled. Thanks to my heat, I was the living, breathing embodiment of a sex pheromone, and it was a testament to his willpower that he didn't start humping me on the spot. My skin flushed, and I couldn't help but wish he'd show a little less restraint.

Maybe if I kissed the hollow of his neck...

I stopped myself just before my lips pressed against his skin.

He'd taken care of me, helped me escape my awful burrow, but he'd never so much as kissed me. I assumed since we'd been best friends since childhood, that he didn't see me as a partner. If I initiated something intimate with him now, he'd be unable to resist. It was basic biology. My shifter nature was doing its best to announce to the world I was ready to breed, and his shifter nature would push him to respond. I couldn't take advantage of him in a moment of weakness.

Fletcher reluctantly released me and got to work unrolling a mattress pad and covering it with blankets. Once he'd finished, he patted the multi-coloured quilt top. "Come on. Get comfy and I'll tell you what's going on with the pack."

Moving onto the pile, I was surprised at how soft the cushioned makeshift bed felt against my aching back. Rolling onto my side, I curled into a ball, all the while working to keep a smile on my face. There was no reason to worry Fletcher with how badly I was handling the contraction-like pains that were gaining strength.

I should tell him to go before I give in and beg him to help relieve my escalating heat. Tears pricked my eyes, hating the idea of being alone. No, that wasn't the real reason. The truth was, I didn't want him to leave me.

Sitting down beside me, Fletcher caught my hand, his thumb rubbing gentle circles on my back. "Monroe wanted to come with me, but as we got close to the cave entrance, we picked up your scent and realized how quickly it had progressed. She didn't want to risk stressing you more by contaminating your space with the smell of another female rabbit."

It was thoughtful, and logically, I appreciated her kindness, but I couldn't ignore the ripple of unease that Fletcher had been near another woman. I knew she had her own fluffle, but that didn't stop me from feeling territorial over the man my inner animal believed was ours.

"The pack has agreed to protect you and allow you to stay here as long as you want. Monroe's mate has two male wolves who are on their way here. They will guard you around the clock." He paused, his mouth opening and closing as though he were struggling with what he planned to say next. "They are, uh… willing to take care of any other needs you have."

He didn't need to spell it out. We both knew exactly what he meant. I probably should've felt shame at the way my core clenched and my body heated at the thought of mating with two complete strangers. For all I knew, they might have been paid for their services.

"She wanted me to tell you they are good men. Gentle wolves with big hearts. As soon as the alpha told them what was happening, they agreed to help."

My brow creased. "That doesn't make sense, Fletcher. Why would they agree to what's basically an arranged marriage to a rabbit shifter they've never met? There has to be something wrong with them, right?"

Then again, beggars can't be choosers. If I wanted to survive this heat without crawling back to my burrow, and they weren't cruel, did it matter what was wrong with them? If they were messy, I was willing to clean. Maybe they snored? I could wear earplugs. And if they chewed too loudly or with their mouths open, I'd learn to deal with it… hopefully.

"All I know is they were unable to find their mates, and they eventually stopped looking. I know you haven't met Monroe, so you don't have any reason to believe her, but I think you can trust her." Fletcher's voice had taken on a croon that was meant to be comforting, but was making my insides feel even more wobbly.

His thumb was still rubbing the back of my hand, and I scooted my hand and his up the blanket until it was mere inches from my face. Giving in to temptation, I rubbed my cheek against his skin. The sharp intake of Fletcher's breath delighted my inner hoe—I mean, *rabbit*.

I'm a good girl. I'm a good girl. I'm a good girl. I chanted the sentence in my mind, trying to remind myself how impor-

5

tant that part of my character had been to me. Not that it helped.

It would be easy to blame my heat for the change, but deep down, I was tired. I longed to let go of the uncertainty that had weighed me down for years and savor life as I took what I desired.

Put simply, I didn't want to be good anymore.

My skin beaded with sweat as lava burned through my stomach and rolled through my veins. Time was running out.

"Fletcher?"

"Yes?" he whispered.

"What if their alpha ordered them to"—I hesitated, my cheeks burning—"to mate with me. We both know that they'll struggle to resist me once they catch the scent of my heat. And it will be too late to warn them by the moment they lick my skin. I don't want to take their right to choose away, which is what will happen if they come in here before I warn them."

A wolf howled in the distance. It was answered a heartbeat later by a second wolf. Their long, eerie calls had my cottontail puckering. These wolves were on our side, but they were predators, and I was prey. There was no way to ignore those facts or my body's instinctual reaction.

Fletcher shifted positions until he could stretch out beside me. We were close enough that I could feel the heat radiating from his fully clothed body.

What would it feel like to press myself against him? Would he push me away?

"Stop those thoughts right now. You're overthinking this and taking on guilt you don't need to feel." Fletcher rested his hand on my hip, giving me a playful shake. "They know. Monroe's mate explained how things work for our kind. They understand the heat, the way females bond for life, your need to be kept safe from anyone who comes looking for you, and they agreed without hesitation. They were given a choice, and they both chose to come of their own free will. Got it?"

He knew the horror I'd feel if I survived my heat, only to discover I'd all but forced two men to take me as their mate.

It took some effort, but I managed to whisper a soft, "Yes."

"Good." His long sigh caused the stray hair around my face to tickle my cheek. "We did it. You're safe, Charlee."

He should have sounded happy, but he didn't. Meeting his gaze, I saw the sadness pooling in their golden depths as he studied my face as though memorizing it for an exam.

Fletcher was leaving.

The ache in my chest had nothing to do with my heat and everything to do with the sudden terror I felt at never seeing him again.

Mine. Just because I wanted him to be mine, it didn't make it so. But how could I let him go without telling him what he meant to me?

My heat became like a living thing, trying to burn my body from the inside out. There was no holding back the cry that was ripped from my chest as fresh agony tore through me. The pair of wolves howled, as though responding. They were closing the distance between us at an alarming pace.

"You're burning up! Crap, crap, crap!" Fletcher sat up, eyes wide as his hands slid over my arms and shirt. "Is this normal? You're completely soaked."

Thanks to the accidental brush of his knuckles against my breasts, it wasn't just my clothing that was soaked. I tried to swallow the whimper that bubbled from my throat, but when Fletcher's hand moved down to my waist, I lost the battle. Unable to hide the raw lust pounding like a bass drum inside me, I moaned.

Moving fast, I wrapped my arms around his neck and pulled his mouth down to mine. Our lips met, and I poured all my emotion into the kiss, wanting him to realize the full depth of how I felt.

Despite the strength my desperation gave me, Fletcher could have easily pulled away. But he didn't. He remained frozen for the span of several moments before his lips moved against mine.

"Don't. Leave. Me," I gasped between kisses.

Fletcher groaned, his muscles trembling. "That's your heat talking."

"You're wrong," I breathed. Shifting my hips slightly, I managed to wrap my legs around his waist and pull him tighter against me. "The heat is just giving me the courage to say what I want."

My breath was coming in short, ragged pants. Between my rising temperature and the lightning-like zap of pain sizzling through my body, the room was beginning to spin. I pulled my lips from his and tried to draw in a deep breath.

Fletcher's fingers dug into my hip, holding my squirming hips still. It wasn't until he stopped me that I noticed his hard length pressed against me. Excitement and hope burst in my chest. He wanted me too.

Or was he just responding like any unmated shifter male would when a woman in heat threw herself at him?

"The plan was to help you escape so you could leave everything in your old life behind. That can't happen if I stay." Fletcher's voice was rough, but I couldn't tell if it was from emotion or the effort of restraining us. "I'm part of your past, Charlee."

"The best part of my past. And yes, the heat is amplifying the raw lust I feel for you—" Bringing my gaze up to meet his, I dropped the walls I hid behind, allowing him to see the bare truth. "But I was already in love with you."

Fletcher's eyebrows drew together as he stared down at me. "You want me to stay?"

"Yes." I worked to keep myself from curling into a ball as my insides twisted and burned.

The heat didn't like being denied. Especially not with an able-bodied male between our legs and separated by nothing but a few scraps of fabric. But I didn't want Fletcher to make his decision based on pity for my current predicament, so I bit down on my tongue to keep from crying out again.

"Oh, Charlee!" The exclamation tumbled from his lips on an exhale as he caught my face between his palms.

This time, he was the one to initiate the kiss—one that would have melted my panties off if I'd been wearing any beneath the ill-fitting sweats.

"You'll stay?" I asked between feverish kisses.

His lips trailed down my neck. "Yes."

There was just one more thing I needed to remind him.

"Fletcher?"

"Hmm?" His tongue teased along my collarbone, making it hard to remember what I was supposed to tell him.

"If we do this…" Even with my body on fire, I could still feel my cheeks heat at what 'this' meant. "I'll bond to you. It's not something I can help. But you don't have to accept me—"

Fletcher brought his mouth back to mine, cutting me off with a surprisingly tender kiss. When he pulled away, he asked, "Will you be my mate, Charlee? I've always known you were the only woman for me."

If he'd told me that a day before, I would have burst into happy tears. But thanks to my raging heat, my response was a single husky word as I ripped away the clothes that were the last thing keeping us apart.

"Mine."

Chapter TWO

CHARLEE

You'd think the fact that I was practically ripping the pants off a man would've been enough to ease my heat and allow me to enjoy bonding with my mate. But I was getting the distinct impression that my inner beast didn't trust me to follow through with what I started. Because instead of easing it, the pain grew more unbearable with each garment tossed to the ground and every brush of his skin against mine.

I tried to shove the bone-melting pain into a box and close the lid, but that was about as effective as trying to nail Jello to the wall. And when Fletcher pulled the oversized cotton shirt over my head, then bent his head to suck the hardened peak of my nipple into his mouth, I couldn't help it. I cried out.

"Did I hurt you?" Fletcher gasped, pulling his head back. "Did I hurt you? Am I going too fast? I'm sorry!"

"No!" I protested, catching his face and practically yanking him back to my chest. "Please don't stop. It's the heat! The longer I keep putting off mating, the more devastating the effects are becoming on my body."

Despite my reassurances, Fletcher hesitated. He placed a gentle kiss on my breast, rather than trying to devour me as he had a moment before.

"The pain isn't going to ease until you've bred me." That was only partially true.

From what I'd been taught, the initial onslaught wouldn't back off until I'd been bred two or three times. Especially since my heat had been brought on early by stress. Worse, I'd delayed mating, rather than asking Fletcher for help sooner. Even after completing the bond with Fletcher, I was going to be in trouble.

As if in response to that, though, another wolf howl echoed down the tunnel, as though assuring me he was coming. He was close, likely only minutes away. My heart skipped a beat, then raced.

It was a very real possibility that the two wolves would race into the cavern, succumb to their predatory instincts, and decide to have rabbit tartar for dinner. I really wanted to take Fletcher as my mate before my untimely death, but time was running out.

"We have the rest of our lives to make love, but I need you inside me." My fingers frantically worked to unbutton the fly of his jeans. "Now."

Fletcher reached between us and undid his stubborn pants.

"I've spent years imagining our first time together, but this wasn't how I'd planned for it to go." The touch of amusement in his tone told me he wasn't upset over the change of plans.

Hooking my thumbs on the waistband of his jeans, I pushed them down as far as I could reach. His erection sprang free as though prepared to slay a monster. I licked my lips at the sight of his pocket sword, beyond ready for a good stabbing.

"Hurry!" I pleaded, shifting my hips to line him up with my slick entrance.

Fletcher buried himself deep inside in a single hard thrust, our voices mingling in a single moan. I'd hoped that once he was filling me, the cramps wracking my body would ease. But those hopes were quickly dashed. Instead, it was as though he'd torn the thin wall that had withheld the full force of my heat.

If I'd been needy before, I was on the verge of desperation now. I growled, fighting the urge to flip Fletcher onto his back and take what my body demanded—anything to ease the turmoil that swelled inside me like a living thing. My nails bit into the palms of my hands from the effort of keeping myself from clawing at his back.

All color seemed to fade from the world around me, and my vision tunneled.

My humanity crumbled away as the simplistic nature of the beast repeated one thought like a loop in my head.

Mate. Mate. Mate.

This was how our species had survived for hundreds of

years—giving in to that animalistic instinct to breed, thus ensuring the future of our kind.

Any hopes or dreams I held as a human didn't matter while my shifter nature was in control. She had one job— make sure I got laid. *Lots.*

Since this was my first heat, I wasn't exactly an expert, but I didn't think what I was feeling was part of the normal experience. With Fletcher's hands traveling across my skin, his mouth on mine, and his hard length filling me, shouldn't I have been elated? Where were the feel-good emotions and delicious sensations I was told would come with my first matings? Why was the dark need roiling beneath my skin going from a shimmer to a boiling liquid?

I was pretty sure I could guess at the reason. Thanks to our harrowing escape, my heat had come early. And with my body fatigued from stress, near starvation, and lack of sleep, I didn't have the physical or mental reserves I needed to handle the heat's demands.

"Faster. Harder," I begged, wrapping my legs around his lower back. "Please."

No longer trusting myself not to bite Fletcher from pain or accidental aggression, I turned my face away from his. Maybe if he filled me, the thing would retreat—or at least let me put a muzzle back on it. For both our safety.

A snarl echoed down the tunnel. The soft thud of heavy paws sent a chill racing down my spine, adding to my already overloaded senses. Even though I knew these wolves had been sent by Monroe to ensure my well-being, I struggled against the instinct to bolt for safety at the approach of a predator.

The two wolves emerged from the dark tunnel, their terrifying shadows stretching up the cave walls thanks to the orb's glow. Fletcher's head snapped toward the entrance, his body motionless. Which totally sucked duck butt, because the instant he stopped moving, agony exploded inside me like a bomb, sending shrapnel slicing through every muscle and organ.

"Fletcher! Don't stop!" I shrieked, tears spilling down my cheeks.

Violent tremors shook my body as I fought the wildness that urged me to take what I needed and make him mine. After all, he wanted me and he'd agreed to this. So where was the problem with making it happen as fast as paranormally possible? Besides, he'd get an orgasm either way.

Great. My beast has lost any semblance of trying to be romantic.

My back arched off the floor as tiny knives seemed to pierce my skin, reminding me I was in a fight for survival. Romance could come later.

Fletcher pushed himself back inside me, his movements wooden and far too slow for my liking as his attention focused on the two predators that circled us. Their sides heaved as they drew in my scent, tasting the air.

One wolf stepped close, flashing sharp canines as his long tongue licked across his muzzle. Each pant sent his hot breath teasing across the skin of my neck and chest. He was so much bigger than I thought a wolf would be, and my lungs deflated as I realized he could rip out my throat before I could utter a single scream. I waited, body trembling from a violent cocktail of the heat and raw terror, to see what the beast would do.

His wet tongue stroked my cheek, roughly licking away the salty tears.

I'm here.

He hadn't spoken the words, but I read them in his eyes.

Chest rumbling with a low snarl, he turned toward Fletcher, the yellow glow of his eyes having nothing to do with the light from the orb.

My heart twisted with a new fear. Just because I was safe, it didn't mean Fletcher would be protected. If they saw him as competition for food or sex, would their beasts drive them to eliminate him?

Reaching up, I wrapped my arms around Fletcher's neck. "He's mine. Don't hurt him!" The words came out as a hoarse, shaky plea rather than the command I'd intended, but I hoped the wolf understood my intent.

"Ah!" Fletcher yelped, jerking forward and driving himself hard into me. "He bit me!"

I moaned in pleasure. Yes. This is what I craved—what I needed.

Then Fletcher's words pierced the fog of lust that clouded my brain. Blinking away the sweat that dripped into my eyes, I caught the glint of eyes behind Fletcher.

The wolf dropped his head, and Fletcher jerked hard, grinding against me. With what remained of my humanity, I knew I should have been worried, but I almost wished the wolf would keep it up and spur Fletcher into action. I needed things to get fast and furious before I lost my tenuous grip on sanity.

"Don't eat him," I whimpered, wanting to protect Fletcher but struggling to form words. "If you have to eat someone, eat me instead."

It was meant to be self-sacrificing, but the image that flashed in my mind was the complete opposite.

"I plan to. Over and over." A low laugh came from the darkness behind Fletcher. "Either finish the job you started or get out of the way, Bunny Boy."

Anger burned away the fear that had lurked in Fletcher's eyes since the wolves had joined us. "Who are you to give me an order? You don't even know her!"

The stranger's laugh was sinfully sexy. "I know that you have your mate in tears and begging for release while you act as though you're on a stroll looking for field mice."

Fletcher snarled something I couldn't make out, then he turned his full attention back to me. This time, his movements were rough, tinged with his anger over having his ability to satisfy me questioned. I should've been upset on his behalf, but I was losing my ability to form cohesive thoughts.

"Yes!" Realizing I'd dug my nails into his shoulders and was likely about to draw blood, I dropped them to my sides.

"There. That wasn't so hard. Was it?" Arrogance dripped from each sarcastic word, something Fletcher no doubt picked up on if his harsh breathing and fingers digging into my hips as he drove himself into me was anything to judge by.

The shift in pace drew another moan from my throat, and my nails dug at the blanket. The wolf nearest my face pushed his massive head beneath my hand, and as though they possessed a mind of their own, my fingers curled into his plush coat, relieved at having something to anchor myself with.

I whimpered as the pleasure in my core wound tighter with each harsh stroke, pushing us ever closer to the precipice. As my gaze locked with Fletcher's, I sucked in my breath at what I saw there.

Love.

"Mine!" I screamed as the first wave of pleasure wove its way through the incessant pain of the heat.

"And you're mine." Fletcher buried himself deep one final time, his body jerking with release.

If he continued speaking, I couldn't hear over the crashing waves of erotic bliss that battered my body. Unfortunately, while I was still trembling through my orgasm, the pleasure was violently shoved aside as my blood turned into a living lava that seared every nerve and muscle.

I hadn't wanted Fletcher to worry after everything he'd risked to help me escape. And until that moment, I thought I'd been doing a good job of hiding just how much trouble I was in. But I'd reached the threshold of what I could bear, and the abrupt escalation was too much to process. My lips parted as I cried.

"Charlee!" Fletcher shouted, pushing away from me, his

eyes scanning my body for injuries. "Did I hurt you? What can I do? Tell me how to help you!"

I couldn't have answered if I'd wanted, because the second he'd pulled his body from mine, I'd lost the ability to do anything other than scream from the agony. That first scream was followed by a second and a third until my throat was raw and my ears rang from the echoing shrieks.

"There's nothing more you can do. Move." The man shouldered past Fletcher. He grabbed my chin in his rough palm, forcing me to look at him. "We both know I came here to mate you while providing protection. But before I do anything, I need to hear the words from your lips. Tell me you want this."

His touch sent lightning sizzling through me.

Mine.

I wasn't sure if it was the heat talking, the pool of desperation I was drowning in, or the tenderness in his brown eyes as his thumb gently stroked my jaw... but I knew I was going to marry this man. And it was going to happen in the next five minutes.

Fine, maybe not marriage in the traditional human sense of the word, but I was going to mate him and tie my heart to him until death did us part.

As I opened my mouth to answer, my muscles seized, sending me into a full-body cramp. My back arched, and unintelligible syllables spilled from my lips.

The fact that the men didn't freak out over my impromptu reenactment of a horror movie exorcism was a testament to their bravery—or confirmation that men would risk it all if there was a chance of getting their willy wet.

The stranger hissed out a curse and slid his right hand under my back, supporting me. His left hand firmly brought my face back to look at him. "Let me help you! Just give me permission."

I wanted to sit down and have a conversation about how our life together would look. What expectations he'd have of his mate. Did he truly understand that I was going to bond with him for the rest of my natural life?

For better or for worse, I was about to hop into an unknown future. One thing was for sure, it couldn't be any worse than the terrible certainty of the future that awaited me if I stayed in the burrow.

The man dropped his head, pressing his face against the side of my neck and drawing my scent deep into his lungs. "Tell me you want this, little rabbit."

"Y-You… are… mine." It was a statement, and a warning. For me, there would be no going back.

The stranger sucked in a harsh breath and his muscles went taut as he held me. It was as though his body shut down as his mind processed my words.

Then, as blood pounded in my ears and pain like a thousand knives seemed to pierce my spine, the man came back to his senses. Raw power rippled around him, and his face settled into a mask of fierce protectiveness. My heat-addled brain couldn't process what had caused it, but my body felt the shift in the air.

Danger. Danger. Danger. Every self-preservation instinct I possessed screamed.

Meanwhile, my ovaries took one look at the crinkle-cut-clit-stick between his legs and exploded in a shower of celebratory confetti. *Yes, please.*

Lifting me so that I straddled his waist and he was cradling me against his chest, my soon-to-be mate's lips brushed against mine for the first time.

"Yes, I'm yours. And you are mine," he murmured. "And never forget it. Because no matter how fast your pretty little tail can hop, you'll never be able to outrun a wolf."

Was that a threat, or a promise of lifetime devotion? I decided it didn't matter as he slid his hand between our bodies, aligning himself with my slick entrance.

As he impaled me on his rigid length, I couldn't even cry out his name... because I didn't know it.

Chapter THREE

COPELAND

Holding my mate in my arms, I struggled to believe it was real and not a dream. She was perfect. Long hair the color of summer wheat framed her heart-shaped face. My mate looked up at me with bedroom eyes the color of a lush spring meadow, stealing my heart and soul on the spot.

When Linc and I had been on our way to help, we knew the female would become our mate. It hadn't mattered in the least what she'd look like. All we needed to know was that she was going through a heat that would likely kill her without intervention, and we would have a mate.

Someone who needed us. Someone to call ours. Someone to love.

Her appearance didn't matter, but one thing had me questioning our compatibility. She was tiny, just like Monroe and Ellora. I'd never ceased being shocked at how small they were compared to wolf shifters. Now, holding the female meant to be mine, I was terrified. Not of lifelong commitment, but of accidentally breaking her.

The alpha and Monroe had explained how heat worked for female rabbits, wanting to make sure we knew Charlee would bond to us during sex. While I was overjoyed to have the gift of a mate drop into my lap, the unfairness of the situation broke my heart.

Charlee wouldn't get to experience the romance of dating and deciding if we were worthy of a one-night stand, let alone men who she wanted to spend the rest of her life with. She had to give her heart and body to strangers in order to survive because her only other choice was death.

"You are mine."

Her words had left me breathless and determined to make sure she never regretted trusting me.

She could've uttered a simple *yes*, giving me permission to assist her during the heat, but she'd done more than that. Charlee claimed me before we had sex, before her rabbit had even bonded to me.

I'd been fighting my wolf for control, barely keeping him from ripping the male rabbit away from our beautiful mate's body. At her words, he forgot all about the male shifter and howled in delight.

She is ours.

Looking into her tear-stained, but trusting face, centuries of shifter energy welled up in my chest.

Mine to protect.

My tongue slid across my bottom lip, pausing at the sweet taste left behind from that soft brush of her mouth against mine.

Mine to love.

Her body trembled, and I moved my hand against her slick skin, trying to better support her. Drawing in a deep breath, I tasted the air, filtering out the sugary fragrance of her heat. The sour scent of fear caused my chest to rumble in displeasure. It was faint, but knowing she was afraid of Linc and I had my heart spasming. It was understandable, even expected, but that didn't stop me from despising the position my mate had been put in. One where she was bonding with a stranger—worse, a beast she instinctively feared.

When the acrid odor of her pain hit me, I forgot all about her lingering fear.

So. Much. Pain.

When experiencing physical trauma, the body released chemicals that were undetectable to humans. For a wolf shifter, those chemicals painted a vivid picture of what the sufferer was going through. Her heat was literally destroying itself from the inside out, and she was hiding it with the strength of a seasoned soldier on a battlefield.

Mine to please.

My hand slid between our bodies. There would be plenty of time for me to rectify the things that had been stolen from my mate. At that moment, I needed to focus on satisfying her beast.

Gripping my cock, I stroked it down her soaked slit.

Charlee's moan sent a ripple down my body as the invisible hair beneath my skin rose.

Satisfied she was wet enough to take me without tearing, I pushed inside her tight heat. Wrapping her arms around my shoulders, she placed kisses across my neck and chest, each more frantic than the last. She was still holding herself back, just as she had with the rabbit male.

Gripping her hips, I ground against her, loving the way her body molded against mine. "You won't hurt me, little rabbit. Wolves have thick skin."

In response, she uncurled her fingers from the tight fists and raked her nails against my skin.

"*Yes*," I hissed, my cock swelling at the delicious sensations stirred by my mate's touch.

My wolf whined as her breathing turned to rapid, shallow pants. Was it from pleasure or pain? Once more, I drew her scent into my lungs, barely suppressing a moan. Did she realize how incredibly intoxicating her scent was? Focusing through the lust, I got my answer. It was both.

My mate was suffering, and I was moving as slowly as the male rabbit had earlier. I could explore her body later, but she needed me to focus on taming her heat.

"Hold on, love." Wrapping my arm around her waist, I lifted her from my length. Just before I sprang free, I thrust my hips upward and brought her down. Hard. Continuing our rhythmic lap dance, I focused on shifting my hips with each stroke, watching her reaction, hoping to find the position that gave her the most pleasure.

Sweat beaded along her hairline and dripped down her

forehead, causing her long blonde hair to stick to her flushed face and neck.

Her petal-pink lips were puffy from being kissed by the male rabbit. Just thinking of him had my chest rattling with a growl.

She was mine.

My fingers slid into her hair and tugged until her head was tilted back, granting me full access to her neck. Trailing my tongue along the pulsing vein beneath her pale skin, I groaned as her flavor danced across my taste buds. I lapped and kissed her neck and skin like a man starved. The urge to mark her pulsed through my skull, but it was a longing I refused to give in to. She was already afraid of me. If I sank my canines into her neck, it could cause her more distress, and that was something I was unwilling to risk. My fingers brushed across the pale white lines that covered much of her back, ribs, and thighs. What horrors had my mate faced?

"Ohhh!" Charlee gasped as I ground our bodies together.

Her nails dug into my skin, holding me close rather than trying to get away. I sucked the sweet sugar from her skin and slid a hand to cup her breast, not once slowing our pace.

"What are you doing?! Stop!" The male rabbit's voice came from somewhere behind me.

A scuffle and a resounding thud followed his protests.

"Do you have a death wish?" Linc snarled.

"He's about to rip her throat out!" the male shouted.

"The only throat in danger is yours, Bunny Boy," Linc warned. "I know you're scared, but take the cotton out of your ears and listen. You're making things worse. For this thing to work between us, you need to sit down and shut up."

His words were harsh, but it was the truth. The situation was volatile and my wolf was ready to kill anyone who dared to get in the way of claiming our mate. We could smell the fear rolling off him, luring us with the promise of a hunt, and any erratic behavior from him would create more issues.

"I... am... fine," Charlee tried to assure him.

Fine? She was just fine? That wouldn't do at all.

Challenge accepted.

Freeing my hand from her hair, I moved it between our bodies. My thumb quickly found its mark, and I was rewarded by the tight spasming of her body around my cock. She whimpered, tightening her legs around my waist and scraping her nails across my back. Her squirming was making it harder to remain in control, and I knew, despite my best intentions, I wasn't going to last much longer.

"Charlee." I tried to focus, something that was impossible with her pretty mouth kissing and nipping my chest.

Her cry of pleasure as she climaxed was the most beautiful sound I'd ever heard. With each pulse of pleasure, her body undulated against mine, her breasts brushing my skin and muscles milking my cock. As much as I loved seeing her enjoy herself, every move of her body brought me closer to my own release. Too close.

"Get her off of you before you hurt her!" Linc's panic sliced through the erotic haze enveloping me like a sandstorm.

"No!" Charlee protested, her voice hoarse.

I tried to open my mouth to speak, to explain why she needed to move away, but words escaped me. All I could think about was the naked beauty pressed against me and how much I wanted to bind us together.

"He's going to swell! If you don't get off him right now, you are going to get stretched. He won't be able to stop it even if you're in pain, and you will be stuck!" Linc's voice rose with a mix of fear and anger.

Charlee's arms tightened around my neck, and my wolf howled in delight. Our mate wasn't ready to leave the safety of my arms. Her stubbornness was adorable.

"Don't touch her," I snapped, flashing my elongated canines at my best friend.

I'd been willing to kill for him before we'd entered the cave. Now I was willing to kill *him*. I would make sure it was a swift and painless death. I wasn't cruel.

Despite not wanting to let go of her, I knew Linc was right. I needed to pull away before the situation got sticky— or more accurately, stucky.

"Charlee, I've got to move you before I—"

"No! You said you're mine. And I want all of you." Her voice trembled, but there was no ignoring her feisty tone.

I could snap her neck faster than she could blink. Yet the tiny rabbit lifted her chin, defiance glittering in her eyes. How was she so freaking adorable?

Her trust that I wouldn't harm her was my undoing. Rocking my hips, I buried myself inside her one final time, hissing as pleasure like nothing I'd ever felt wracked my entire being.

Charlee moaned as the swelling stretched her tight channel, rubbing every overly sensitive secret place she possessed.

"Are you okay?" I croaked, my tight throat making it hard to speak. "If you can relax, it will hurt less."

"Compared to the worst of the heat, this is pure bliss." She trembled and rested her forehead against my chest.

Scenting the air, I hummed in approval when I found the scent of her pain had nearly dissipated. It was temporary, and I knew it would be back, but for now, the demands of her heat had been satisfied.

I leaned back against the cave wall, barely noticing the jagged stones digging into my back. As gently as I could, I adjusted her so that she lay on my chest.

"You have to stop moving," she gasped.

"Why is that, little rabbit?" I asked, barely hiding my smile.

Her soft pants and the way her body trembled had already given me the answer, but I wanted to hear her tell me.

"It's just… every time you move, it causes me to…" she huffed. "I-I just didn't realize it was possible to climax this many times in a row."

"Such an innocent little rabbit," I chuckled. "When you

aren't suffering through a heat, I can't wait to show you just how many times I can make you come in one night."

Judging by the strangled sound from her throat and the way her body clenched around my cock, she liked that idea. A lot.

"Close your eyes and rest while you can." Holding her close, I stroked a hand down her slick, sweat-soaked hair. "You're safe."

Chapter FOUR

CHARLEE

T hose precious hours of sleep were a much-needed break from the nightmare of my heat. I cried out as I was roused from the bliss of nothingness by violent spasms that caused my aching muscles to contort all over again. A large hand moved across my hip to rub my lower back, sending electricity sizzling across my skin.

My heart rate spiked as memories of the night before flashed through my mind. When my eyelids fluttered open and my vision cleared, I'd expected to find Fletcher's eyes, or those of the wolf who'd coaxed me to sleep. Instead, I found an unfamiliar set of golden eyes watching me.

"Hello, sugar." A slight southern drawl to his words caused my stomach to wobble like those tall Jello monstrosities that came from a cake mold.

"Hi—" My greeting turned to a hiss as knives stabbed at my internal organs.

Crap! If I didn't want to experience the full brunt of the heat, I needed to take a quick hop to Pound Town.

"The pain is back." He made it a statement, not a question.

I nodded in acknowledgement, then stopped as the room spun.

Warmth radiated from his palm as he rubbed my back, seeping into my skin like a hot water bottle. I wished I could tell him how nice it felt, but I was too focused on controlling my breathing to carry on a conversation.

"How can I help?"

A snort escaped before I could swallow it. We both knew the only thing that was going to get me through this hellish experience.

Instead of being offended, the man laughed, tiny lines appearing around his eyes. "Yeah. That was a stupid question."

I wanted to laugh with him and get lost in his smile, but my inner shifter had no patience for romance. My temperature spiked, and my heart rattled against my ribs until I could hear nothing over the roar of blood in my ears. To my absolute horror, my body seemed to take on a life of its own, arching against him as though announcing that fast food wasn't the only thing that came hot and ready.

"Mmm," he hummed in appreciation.

His fingers dug into my back, hauling me against him,

allowing me to feel his hard length burning my belly. I was left with no doubts about his readiness to serve.

Rather than throwing myself at yet another stranger, I probably should've searched for Fletcher or my first wolf mate. But there was a reason my rabbit's favorite holiday was Christmas… because she was an absolute *ho, ho, ho.*

The man was willing, and we were able. Apparently, that was all that mattered when you were in heat.

My leg slid over his hip, positioning myself so his erection rested against my slit. It wouldn't take much to angle my hips and let him slide in…

"A woman who knows what she wants is such a turn-on." His hand moved from my back to cup my butt.

The blanket slid down to our waists, exposing me to his hungry gaze.

He was right. I knew what I wanted, but the past twenty-four hours had been the most awkward of my life. Nothing about the situation was comfortable or normal.

As though sensing my thoughts, the man switched my position in a move so smooth I thought it must have been magic. My back now pressed against his chest while I faced a sleeping Fletcher.

"You can ask him to breed you. He fell asleep when you did and hasn't moved a muscle since."

"Fletcher hasn't slept much since we escaped. He stayed awake to guard me," I whispered, noting the dark circles beneath his eyes. "He needs to save his energy."

Rabbit males weren't built to breed a female back-to-back. It was why females needed a fluffle to get them through a full heat. With the added stress of getting me to safety, he needed to rest. But the pain wasn't going to wait, and I bit my lip to keep from screaming and waking him.

"Do you want me?" The wolf shifter's mouth teased along the curve of my ear.

"Yes." It was the truth.

Heat or not, I wouldn't have had the strength to refuse what he was offering. Who could have blamed me? With his tanned skin, the 5 o'clock shadow on his square jaw, and messy brown hair, he looked as though he spent his days working cattle and riding horses. He even had the calloused palms and farm-earned muscles to finish the look.

Yep. The man was sexy as sin, and every woman on earth would've had lifelong regrets if she turned down an opportunity like that one.

A hand slid over my hip and down to the apex of my thighs. His fingers rested against me, not moving, but still driving me crazy.

"If we mate, I might want to keep you," he teased.

"Cool, cool." I gasped as he dipped a single finger inside me.

"Sugar, you are so wet." He slipped a second finger inside me.

I could do nothing but whimper as he stroked, slowly at first but picking up speed until he found the rhythm that drove me wild. My hips twitched, seeking friction as my release coiled tighter with each pump of his fingers.

"It's a shame all that sweet cream is being wasted." His

mouth sucked and nipped along my neck. "I can't wait to spend a night between your legs, savoring your taste."

That was all it took. I moaned as a stranger's touch gave me the most intimate of pleasures. Despite my efforts to be quiet, Fletcher's eyes opened, locking with mine, and then the wolf behind me.

"What's going on?" His voice was husky with sleep.

"Kiss her," the wolf ordered, not bothering with niceties or even simple courtesy.

Fletcher didn't need to be told twice. Rolling toward me, the men sandwiched me between their bodies. I nearly whined at the loss of the man's fingers, but it changed to a moan as he buried himself inside me. Fletcher's mouth captured my moans as the wolf's hips rocked, stretching and stroking every hidden inch of me.

My cheeks burned with feverish need and embarrassment over how turned on I was by the situation. A stranger's cock was filling me and his fingers had returned to add delicious friction, while Fletcher, my lifelong crush, sucked my bottom lip as his hand cupped my aching breast. It was dirty and beautiful all at the same time, and I was greedily taking everything they offered me.

When Fletcher's thumb flicked across my nipple, I arched into him, pushing my butt back against the wolf. He responded with a groan, his hips grinding against me as he thrust deep. He trailed kisses along my bare shoulders, and although he tried to be discreet, I caught the swirl of his tongue as he greedily lapped at the sweet aphrodisiac that coated my skin.

I had to hand it to the men. They made a great team, and they were learning how to bring me to climax faster with each coupling. It was a good thing when it came to sating the demands of my heat, but I worried about my long-term stamina when the heat was over.

"I'm going to—" Pleasure erupted, stealing away my breath before I could complete my sentence.

Fletcher caught my chin, drinking in my face. "You're so beautiful."

As I fought to keep my heavy-lidded eyes open, I wondered if he'd think the same if I lost the battle to keep my eyes from crossing. Combined with the drool caused by their hot bodies and the crazy bed-hair all around my face, I was sure I looked super attractive.

"Charlee, do you want me to pull out?" The wolf's words were harsh, and his breathing was coming in ragged pants.

"No. Stay." I didn't even need to think about the answer. Sliding my hand down, I interlaced my fingers with his and rested them against my stomach.

The man tightened his arm around me, as though he were trying to merge us into one being. The fragrance of towering oak trees and moss-covered earth enveloped me. His body dwarfed mine, and the muscles in his arms flexed with restrained power, yet he held me with such gentleness.

For a moment, the demands of my shifter nature disappeared, allowing me to experience the comforting warmth of his embrace. "I want all of you."

"How long?" His words were soft, his voice smooth as whiskey.

"What?" I asked, not understanding his question.

"How long do you plan to keep me?" There was a lonely note in his voice that nearly broke my heart.

He knew I'd be bonded to him for life. Didn't he? Yet, he was still worried I'd reject him. That I wouldn't want him.

"Forever," I whispered. "You're mine."

His hot breath tickled my hair as he released the breath he must've been holding. "Yours."

The man's hips rocked against me once more, burying himself deep and finding his own release. My belly tightened with growing need as he swelled inside me, massaging and rubbing every inch of my tight channel.

Fletcher scooted down until his mouth was level with my breasts. His tongue swirled around my nipple, teasing and sucking until stars sparkled in my vision and my belly was heavy with the need for release. My body quivered with chills that swung wildly between lava hot and polar ice.

I squirmed, trying to escape the terrifying power of the frantic desire demanding release. "It's too much! I'm going to pass out!"

"Let go." The wolf's mouth traveled up my neck toward my ear.

Was he crazy? It was like telling me to sky dive without a parachute.

"I can't!" What if it tore me apart and I couldn't put myself back together?

"You can." Fletcher's hand caught my chin, forcing me to meet his gaze. "Come for us."

And for the first time in my life, I obeyed a command.

There, in the safety of my hastily thrown together nest, between two men I'd tied myself to for the rest of my life, I leaped from the precipice into the tumultuous ecstasy, trusting them to catch me.

I'd never felt safer.

"Let her sleep!"

"She needs to eat."

"If you interrupt her sleep, I'll turn you into a dog toy!"

"You don't have a dog!"

"I'll get one! Now shut up before you wake her!"

"What's your plan? Wait until the pain wakes her up again and she can't eat? Our mate can't live on sex alone."

I'm willing to give it a try... The corner of my mouth twitched.

"I'm serious, man! Wake her up and I'll kill you in your sleep tonight."

Fletcher spoke up for the first time. "He's joking. Right?"

"No," the wolves answered in unison.

Fletcher laughed nervously, trying to ease the tension. "Do things with you two always escalate this fast?"

He'd always been a peacemaker. His gentle spirit was rare in our burrow, where males seemed to thrive on competition and domination.

"Fine. How about you hold her while I feed her?" my first wolf mate offered in compromise.

The muscles in the arm I was tucked beneath flexed as though preparing to choke whoever came within striking distance. "Wake her and your fate is sealed, buttsniffer."

I bit my lip to keep from laughing, thankful the blanket partially covered my face.

"Take it outside. There isn't enough room in here for a dogfight," Fletcher huffed. "Besides, she's already awake."

The wolf lifted the blanket, peering beneath it. His eyes softened. "Well, hello there, sugar."

"Hi." Despite the intimacy we'd shared and the fact that my naked body was pressed against his, my heart skipped a beat, and a flush spread across my cheeks.

He is so doggone cute. Or is it wolfgone cute?

Reaching up, I brushed the hair from where it had fallen over one of his eyes. Sun-kissed golden strands wove through his messy brown hair. It wasn't long enough to tie back, but it was the perfect length to run your fingers through… and grip during sex.

Mind out of the gutter, Charlee! I mentally scolded myself.

They were supposed to be the canines, but I was the one acting like a horndog.

Catching my hand, he brought it to his mouth and kissed each finger. Every touch of his lips did crazy things to my belly, and I forgot to breathe.

"Oh no you don't," the first wolf snapped.

He yanked the blanket away and scooped me into his arms. "I know that look, and our mate is going to eat before you corrupt her any further."

Glancing back at the golden-eyed wolf, I watched him cross his arms behind his head, not even attempting to hide himself. At his husky laugh, my eyes snapped up to his face. A wicked smirk slid across his face. He'd caught me staring, and we both knew it.

"I can take it all the way off if you want, sugar." He winked, causing butterflies to take flight in my stomach.

"Have you no shame, Linc?" the wolf holding me grumbled.

"Linc," I breathed, testing the name.

"I like hearing you say my name." Linc's brazen, almost daring expression shifted to something more vulnerable. "Technically, it's Lincoln, but no one calls me that."

"Okay. Then Linc it is." I smiled.

At least now I know what name to scream the next time he brings me to the Big O.

The wolf holding me choked, and Linc barked out a laugh.

Back the truck up! Did I say that out loud?

A quick glance at the wolfish grin on Linc's face gave me my answer. My cheeks burned, but I couldn't deny my attraction to him. If I'd been Little Red Riding Hood, I would have purposely taken a detour from grandma's house and begged this wolf to have his way with me.

The man sat down, pulling me down on his lap. In an

effort to distract them from my lack of a filter, I twisted around to look up at him. "And your name is?"

"Just call me yours," he rumbled, dipping his head to kiss the tip of my nose.

"Okay, Yours." My nose twitched as I sniffed the air. "What did you bring me to eat? I'm starved!" As if it were a paid actor, my stomach growled loudly.

His eyebrows shot up to his hairline. "Thought you were a rabbit shifter? If you ask me, it sounds like you have an inner wolf you're trying to hide."

"Maybe you just don't know how scary rabbits can be," I teased, enjoying my mate's laugh.

"I guess you're right. Honestly, the idea of the Easter Bunny always creeped me out." He fake shuddered, then smiled. "My name is Copeland. And I wasn't sure what you liked to eat, so I brought a bit of everything."

Unable to resist the urge, I leaned forward and touched my lips to his jaw. "I like just about everything."

"Charlee may be a rabbit, but she doesn't eat like one," Fletcher teased.

My gaze slid over him, relieved to find some color had returned to his pale face. While he still cast quick glances between the wolves, most of the tension in his muscles had eased.

As if reading my thoughts, Fletcher leaned forward to squeeze my hand. "We're safe and we're together."

"And most importantly, we have a family." I blinked away my tears and tried to smile. "I don't even care if we have a house. I'm pretty fond of this cave."

Copeland wrapped me in a gentle embrace. "Yes. A family." He buried his nose in my hair and nuzzled the top of my head.

Linc cleared his throat. "And for the record, we do have a house. Now feed our woman before her inner wolf breaks free and devours us all."

Chapter FIVE

CHARLEE

S tretching my arms above my head, I stared at the three men lying in a tangled heap on the blanket pile. They were so exhausted after spending the past three days making sure I stayed stuffed full of soup and their man meat, that they hadn't even noticed when I climbed out from between them.

Linc had fallen asleep holding a sandwich that was now mashed against his face. Barely stifling a snicker, I watched as Copeland rolled over and spooned Fletcher. Both men were going to be pretty upset when they woke up and realized they were cuddling. I couldn't wait.

Thanks to their valiant efforts, they'd sated the heat enough that I'd been able to sleep for several hours before my temperature had spiked and I'd woken drenched in sweat. My inner slut was up early and already stoking the fires of my heat. Resting a hand against my churning stomach, I breathed through a cramp.

How long before I have to wake one of my mates and find release? Probably not very long...

Deciding I needed to make the best of the limited time I had, I padded to the corner of the cave where Copeland had stacked supplies. I found the toothbrush and toothpaste Copeland had brought along with the food. After brushing my teeth, I ran a comb through my tangled hair.

What I really wanted was a shower, but the wet wipes would have to do. Realistically, I wouldn't be comfortable leaving my nest for several more days. But maybe there was a water source nearby where we could take a quick dip? I decided to ask the wolves when they woke.

Needing a snack, but not wanting to wake my mates with the sound of crinkling wrappers, I tiptoed my way outside.

The moment I emerged into the late afternoon sun, every hair on my body rose, standing on end. Tendrils of smoke drifted between the thick tree trunks of the surrounding forest, creeping ever closer to the cave entrance.

Don't freak out, Charlee. Maybe someone is camping? Or maybe it's another gender reveal gone wrong, and the firefighters will have it under control within minutes.

As I took a deep breath, hoping to calm my frayed nerves, a new scent caught my attention. It was faint, almost entirely hidden by the acrid odor of burning wood.

But there was no mistaking who—or rather, *what*—it belonged to.

Coyotes.

The cave was on pack lands, although just barely, since we hadn't been willing to venture too far across the boundary before receiving permission from the alpha to stay. Still, it would be suicide for coyotes to venture close enough that I could pick up their scent. Needing to make sure I hadn't imagined it, I took another deep whiff, coughing as the thickening smoke filled my lungs.

Predator.

Instincts that had passed from grandparent to parent to child kicked in.

Run! Do not pass go and do not collect $200. Move!

The scent seemed to be coming from all directions, so my best bet was to head left and get a head start. The cave wasn't an option, because they could follow and I'd be pinned. But as my muscles tightened to obey the primal survival instinct and disappear into the brush, I hesitated. My mates were in the cave, and if caught unaware, they'd be in danger.

Run. Run. Run.

The demand drummed in my skull, demanding that I obey. Rabbits survived predators one of two ways: outrun our would-be murderers, or run until we find a hole to dart inside that was too small for the predator to follow.

Fighting my instincts, I tripped backward into the entrance of the cave. I had to warn them, even if it meant being trapped.

I flew through the tunnel. "Get up!"

The men remained motionless. What the warren was wrong with them?

Why hadn't they heard me scrambling through the tunnel?

Maybe I killed them. Is this what they meant by a body count? I was like a freaking dragon, but instead of gold, I was collecting penises! Pull yourself together, Charlee!

"Get up!" I hissed, leaping on top of the guys and shaking them. "Coyotes are coming, and the woods are on fire!"

The three men bolted upright so fast that I fell backward, screaming and grabbing my chest in shock.

"Are you sure?" Fletcher asked, pulling me back into a sitting position.

"Y-Yes," I whisper-shouted. "They are close, but still a little way off. I think. Ugh! Rabbits don't exactly stop to see how close a predator is, so for all I know, they're right outside. We have to run if we're going to escape them! *Now!*"

Linc snorted, pushing to his feet. "Run? Wolves don't run; we fight."

"We need to know how many coyotes we are facing," Copeland added. "And you are going to stay in the cave where it is easier to defend you."

Both wolves ducked, disappearing into the tunnel. Fletcher and I held our breath until they reappeared. One look at the grim set of their jaws and my stomach plummeted to my toes.

"The smoke makes it hard to pinpoint the exact number of unique scents, but I'm guessing there are nearly thirty coyotes. Possibly more." Copeland stared back down the tunnel entrance, prepared should anyone try to sneak inside.

"They are too close to risk trying to get Charlee to safety. If they surrounded us, it would be too hard to fight and try to keep her from getting caught in the crossfire." Linc ran a hand through his hair and cursed. "I've already alerted the alpha, and wolves are on the way."

"I thought the alpha said wolves would patrol near the cave? So, it shouldn't be long before they arrive, right?" Fletcher asked, giving my arm a reassuring squeeze.

"They were, but a wildfire broke out on the far side of the pack lands. It spread so fast that it burned several homes. The full pack is working to put it out and evacuate the rest of the houses in the danger zone." Linc's jaw clenched and unclenched.

"It was a setup to draw security away from us," Fletcher stated the obvious.

"It would seem so. But what the coyotes want with either of you, I don't know. Nothing about this makes sense," Copeland muttered.

"I'll explain later. But this is definitely our burrow's doing." Fletcher moved toward the pile of tattered clothing, tossing them aside until he found the shirt I'd worn.

Linc began barking out orders. "I will hold them off at the entrance. Copeland will stand just inside the tunnel, and Fletcher will be the third line of defense."

I finally found my voice. "More than thirty? And how many coyotes can a wolf take on?"

"You don't need to worry. We'll keep you safe." Copeland turned from watching the tunnel, his eyes glowing.

"How many? I want a realistic answer," I demanded.

"Around five. It is tough to estimate since it depends on the condition of the wolf and the coyotes. Your guys can probably handle a few more, but to take on that many coyotes, they'll need the strength of the pack," Fletcher answered, lifting my shirt and ripping off one sleeve.

All three of our heads snapped in his direction. How could he know that?

"Which means they will severely maim or kill Copeland and Linc before backup can arrive," Fletcher added as he moved to my side and began rubbing the shirt sleeve all over my body.

"What are you doing?" I batted at his hands and tried to step back. "This is a weird time to try to clean me!"

"Be still!" Fletcher's barked command shocked me into obeying. He'd never been stern with me. "I'm going to shift, and you are going to rub my fur against your skin. Then you are going to slip this sleeve around my body."

"But why—" My blood turned to ice as I realized what he was planning. "Fletcher! You can't! If they catch you—"

"They won't. We both know I'm faster." He placed a tender kiss against my lips. "I'm no help in hand-to-teeth combat, but I can run."

Stepping away from me, he turned to the wolves. "I'll

run along the ridge and cut back toward the pack house. Tell the pack my plan so I don't end up a wolf snack. If we're lucky, some of them will follow my trail, thinking I'm Charlee. That should give you two better odds."

Respect shone in the wolves' eyes while tears shimmered in mine.

"Protect her."

"You have our word." Linc took Fletcher's forearm in a warrior's grip. "Run with the speed of your ancestors, Bunny Boy."

Linc's insulting nickname broke through the tension, and Fletcher chuckled.

Without another word, he shifted forms. I quickly kneeled and rubbed his soft fur against my skin. Once the shirt sleeve had been slipped around his body, I held him in front of my face.

"Come back to me, my love." Touching my nose to his, I set him on the ground and tried not to sob as he darted down the tunnel.

"I'm going to the entrance to listen and get an idea of how many follow him." Linc disappeared the moment he finished speaking.

Copeland grabbed Fletcher's shirt and tossed it to me. "Put this on. The more we can mute your scent, the better."

I pulled it over my head without argument, thankful to be wrapped in my mate's comforting scent. My insides churned as dizziness made the room spin. Fight to the death or not, my heat wasn't planning on giving me even a brief intermission from the pain.

How long before my scent bloomed and became stronger as it attempted to seduce any male with a nose who happened to be within sniffing distance?

Copeland stroked my hair, although whether it was to calm me or him, I couldn't tell. "I'm going to shift. If I need to fight, I'm stronger in that form."

At my nod of acceptance, he moved away from me, shifting quickly to his chocolate wolf. Moving to the back of the cave, I curled into a ball on my side.

"It worked! At least a dozen coyotes followed Fletcher. I will hold off the entrance. If any slip by, I'll bark a warning." Linc didn't wait for my response before shifting and bolting back into the tunnel.

Copeland padded to where I lay and collapsed on top of me, his giant body nearly covering me entirely. I knew he was trying to smother my scent, but my heat didn't get the memo. My mate was so close, I could ask him to shift back. We could make it quick...

What the freak is wrong with me?

Coyotes were literally about to assault the cave's entrance, and I was more focused on convincing Copeland to torpedo *my* cave's entrance. Closing my eyes, I focused on slowing my heartbeat and breathing through the cramps.

Linc's howl had every hair on my body standing on end. It wasn't the reassuring call it had been that first day as they'd been on their way to my side. Nor was it the hauntingly beautiful song that wolves sang to the moon.

This was a battle cry; the wolf version of one: *"Come and get it, boys."*

Wild yips from the coyotes followed Linc's taunting howl. Each bark brought them closer until they had to be near the entrance. That suspicion was confirmed when a vicious growl rang out, followed immediately by the pained cry of a coyote.

The fight had begun.

Chapter SIX

CHARLEE

The cave shook as bodies slammed against the entrance, and the tunnel amplified the chilling snarls until it seemed like I was in the middle of the brawling beasts outside. Smoke rolled into the cave, bringing the coppery scent of blood and the stench of unbathed coyotes. It was becoming harder to breathe with each passing second.

Biting down on my knuckle, I tried to muffle my cries. Copeland whined and licked at the tears streaking down my cheek. As the heat of the battle and my body escalated, I split my focus between trying to hold off my bunny's demands and straining to hear Linc's growls, needing to know he was still alive.

How much longer before the pack showed up? More importantly, how long could Linc hold off the coyotes before he was too exhausted and got injured?

My answer came minutes later when Linc howled in pain. A sharp warning bark had Copeland leaping off me and bounding into the dark tunnel.

Lifting my head, I listened as Copeland's vicious snarl filled the chamber. A coyote tried to respond, but his bark was abruptly cut off, and the cave trembled as something collided with the wall.

Was Linc injured? Dead? I hadn't heard a sound from him since he'd called Copeland into the fray.

A second agonizing bark tore at my heart, causing all the self-control I'd summoned to evaporate. I'd shoved my heat into a mental box and had been barely holding the lid closed, but with my concentration broken, the box exploded as though it held a bomb. My temperature spiked, burning me alive from the inside out. I tried to move, but none of my muscles would obey. Gasping, I struggled to inflate my lungs, sucking in the dense, foul-tasting air.

All I wanted to do was curl into a ball and sob until the nightmare was over, but I couldn't sit there listening as my mates died defending me. There had to be something I could do.

Scanning the cave, my gaze landed on the silverware Copeland had brought for me. A steak knife. It wasn't my first choice of a weapon, but it was one I'd used before. I shuddered, trying not to think about how that had ended.

I pushed to my knees, crawling until I could snatch the knife off the ground. Using the protruding stones that lined the cave wall, I pulled myself to my feet and staggered toward the tunnel. Each step felt like I was moving through quicksand that was intent on dragging me down.

The room tilted back and forth like a nauseating teeter-totter, sending bile rushing up my throat. My knees wobbled, refusing to hold my weight. Collapsing to the stone floor, I swallowed my scream of frustration.

I couldn't give up. My mates needed me. Nothing else mattered.

A low growl had my head snapping up. I was fully prepared to come face-to-face with a mouthful of coyote teeth. Instead, I found Linc's wolf towering over me. He growled again, dropping his head as though preparing to charge.

One look at the glowering wolf was all it took to spur me into action. I didn't even bother to stand, but crab-walked backward.

Linc matched my every move, forcing me back into the cave. His upper lip curled as he bared his glistening white fangs at me. I knew this man was my mate, the one who swore to protect me, but catching sight of the blood dripping from his jaws, I could no longer silence the voices—or more accurately, the screams—of my ancestors.

With the surge of adrenaline coursing through my blood, I rolled to my stomach and pushed to my knees in a single, smooth move. My muscles tightened as I bolted, intent on escaping the snarling predator.

Where I was planning to go to get away from him, I didn't know. Fight, flight or freeze was in control, and all I knew was I was going to fly like I'd been born with wings.

And fly I did… like I was a freaking penguin.

I'd only made it a few feet when I face-planted on the pile of blankets, thanks to Linc's massive wolf tackling me from behind.

Since flying wasn't happening, I went with plan B: play dead.

Some predators liked to play with their food and grew bored if their dinner didn't give them a show first. I just hoped Linc's wolf was that type of predator.

Closing my eyes, I lay perfectly still, not daring to even breathe. A cold nose poked my butt cheek and then my back as the wolf moved to stand over me. His soft fur brushed my bare skin, a shocking contrast to the rough, wet tongue that ran along my ribs.

What the buck?

Was he checking to see if my ribs would make a nice appetizer? Fury pushed aside some of my terror. If my mate was going to eat me for disobeying one little order, maybe I'd shift into my rabbit form and turn myself into a bite-sized snack. It would serve him right if he got less meat!

Hot air blew against the back of my neck, making it hard to stick with my pretend-to-be-roadkill plan. I whimpered as Linc's jaws wrapped around my neck, his sharp teeth pressing into my skin. Still, I remained motionless, not wanting to antagonize a wolf who held my future—or lack thereof—in his jaws.

As if recognizing the opportunity to make me as miserable as possible, a spasm caused my entire middle to contract. Pressing my face into the blanket, I gritted my teeth and hissed through the agonizing contraction. Just when I was about to ask the wolf to do a quick chiropractic adjustment on my neck and put me out of my misery, he released me.

Instead of leaving, he continued using his weight to pin me down. He was careful not to hurt me, but enough to get his point across. Move, and he'd be on me faster than a rabbit to a garden.

A single wolf howled in the distance, and Copeland responded with a call of his own. It was answered by another wolf and then a third... and fourth. A heartbeat later, the silence was filled with an army of howls.

Linc lifted his head and joined in the war cry of his pack. It was like nothing I'd heard before and sent chills racing from my toes to my scalp. Even if I lived for a thousand years, I knew I'd never forget the masterpiece composed by a unified pack protecting their land and family.

Logically, I knew I was safe with the pack, but with survival instincts ruling my mind and body, I couldn't help but tremble in terror at the wolves' savage serenade. I wanted to know how badly Linc had been hurt, if Fletcher had made it to safety, and to make sure Copeland was unharmed. But the crescendoing pain made it impossible to get my scattered thoughts into coherent sentences, let alone get to my feet.

The air crackled with static, and Linc's weight eased on top of me. Instead of fur, bare skin brushed mine.

"Why do I smell fear, little mate?" Even though it was his stubble-covered jaw nuzzling against my cheek, there was a roughness to his voice that hadn't been there before. Just how close was his wolf to the surface? "The pack is here to protect us."

"To protect you and Copeland," I croaked, my throat dry. "I'm a stranger to them."

It didn't matter to me why they'd answered the call; I was beyond grateful for their presence.

"Wrong. They came to protect you, too. You and Fletcher are family."

"Okay, Dom." The words were out before I could stop them. I couldn't help that sarcasm was my coping mechanism for pain.

"Dom?" Linc's hand slid under my hip, flattening against my stomach. "Are you into the BDSM stuff?"

"BDSM?" I racked my deep-heat-fried-brain trying to figure out the acronym.

Boy Don't Sniff Me?

Bouncy Dicks Stab Me?

Bunny Does Sexy Men?

Beast Dudes Savor Me?

Bombastic Dicks Slay Mate?

Frankly, I liked the sound of every option my brain could come up with. "I'm not sure. Maybe? Dom is from a movie about fast cars. He's obsessed with family."

Linc hummed in acknowledgement, his mouth busy sucking and kissing down my neck. Liquid heat rushed between my legs, and my fingers curled into the blanket.

Yesss! This is exactly what I need. No, wait!

"Linc, are you hurt?" I tried to twist around to check for myself, but received a warning growl for my efforts.

"Yeah. I'm so hard it hurts." Rocking his hips, Linc's erection slid against my butt, letting me feel the truth of his words. "How about I make us both feel better?"

"What about Copeland? Fletcher?" Desperate to accept what he was offering, I wiggled my behind, trying to give him better access.

"They are fine. Now stop thinking." Using the palm pressed to my belly, he lifted me from the blanket.

I barely had time to register his cock bumping against my soaked entrance before he buried himself inside me. Pinned to the floor, there was little I could do other than cry out his name as he took me hard from behind.

This wasn't gentle lovemaking. It was raw, animalistic sex. A testosterone-filled warrior male claiming the reward of having protected his woman. And my inner shifter was eating it up… not that I had any complaints either.

Chills ran along my skin as Linc's free hand brushed against my ribs, moving upward until he could cup my breast. The roughened skin of his thumb teased my nipple, causing my channel to spasm around his length.

"Linc!" It was all I could say as the man pounded our bodies together, driving us faster and faster toward the precipice.

"Mine," he murmured, his mouth trailing kisses over my shoulder.

"I'm yours." My eyes crossed as pleasure began rippling through me.

"Tell me." He punctuated the order with a hard thrust of his hips.

It took me a minute to understand what he wanted me to say. "You're mine."

His hand moved down from my breast until it slid between my legs. "Say it again."

The man was asking a lot of me. I was struggling to remember my name, let alone what we were talking about only moments before.

"Linc, you belong"—I gasped as his finger began stroking my clit—"to me."

"Um-hmm." His steady rhythm had me whimpering with the need for release.

"Mine for today and forever," I assured him as blood pounded in my ears.

"Charlee, I want to mark you." His voice was rough, but his words were so soft it took me a heartbeat to understand what he'd said.

"Then mark me."

For the first time, he stumbled, missing a beat with his steady thrusts. "It means biting you. And I don't want to scare you."

The man could have ripped me apart when he'd found me in the tunnel with a knife. He'd had enough control to keep that from happening. I wasn't scared anymore.

"Mark me."

Linc's cock jerked inside me and his chest rumbled with a sound that wasn't quite human. His beast was close.

There was no warning before his teeth sank into my

neck, but the instant they pierced my skin, my orgasm exploded like a grenade. My body tightened around Linc's erection, squeezing him until he was jerking hard inside me. The sounds of our pleasure filled the cave as he swelled, locking us together.

As we lay there, catching our breath and basking in the afterglow of sex, the soft thud of approaching paws came down the tunnel. I stiffened. Had a coyote somehow snuck past the wolves? Was someone from the pack about to find us naked?

"Relax. It's Copeland," Linc assured me, his words muffled against my neck.

Blinking in the dim light, I watched a brown wolf step out of the shadows. His tail swished across the floor as he moved close, presenting me with something that hung from his mouth.

"GREAT LOPPING LAPIN! You killed Fletcher!" I screamed, trying my best to scoot out from under Linc's body.

"Sugar, calm down—"

Dropping the bundle of slobber-covered black and white fur next to my face, Copeland lay down on his belly and whined.

"Or what? You'll eat me too?" I demanded, struggling as he tried to hold me still.

Things were about to get real Watership Down in that cave, if you know what I mean. But the furball sat up with a grunt. Eying Copeland, he sat back on his hind feet and pulled an ear between his front paws as he tried to clean the wet fur.

I choked on a sob. "You're alive!"

Linc snorted. "Of course he is. We aren't monsters. Bunny Boy was too exhausted to make it back to the cave. Copeland went to retrieve him because he thought you'd rest better if you had all your mates here."

Copeland stared up at me and whined again.

Well, great. Guilt hit my stomach like acid, and my eyes burned. I should've been thanking him, not accusing him.

"I'm sorry, Copeland." Reaching out, I tried to brush his cheek, but he was just out of reach.

To my relief, the wolf scooted closer and rubbed his face against my palm. His tail swished the floor, stirring up dust. But I didn't care. I was too happy to have my mates with me to care about the crappy air quality in the cave.

Linc rolled us so that we lay on our sides, my back still tight against his chest and his erection still filling me. "Copeland said the pack is stationed around the cave. They will keep guard tonight to give us time to rest before we have to move."

I chewed my lip, hating the idea of leaving my nest, but knowing it couldn't be helped.

Fletcher finished grooming himself and ducked under my arm so he could tuck himself against me. As he stretched out, I did my best not to laugh at the way his fur stuck out in random patches.

Copeland had shifted during my distraction and lay down as well, sandwiching me between my two wolf mates.

"I'm sorry—"

"Don't start that again. Go to sleep." Copeland kissed my forehead, then lay back and closed his eyes. "But if you decide to have sex again, keep it down. I could hear the two of you over the fight—"

"The whole pack heard us?" I whisper-shrieked.

"Yes." Copeland chuckled. "How could they not?"

"Then I hope you were planning on us moving far, far away. How can I look them in the eye when I meet them?"

"Proudly." Linc nipped at my neck. "That's how I plan to do it. Let them be jealous of how my mate pleases me."

Chapter SEVEN

CHARLEE

I fought to keep the drool in my mouth as Copeland stood and stretched. "I hate to stress you when you're sleeping so well, but we need to consider getting a move on."

A yawning pit opened in my stomach, and my mouth went dry. Move where?

My thoughts spun at a dizzying pace. How angry was the alpha over the attack? I'd brought trouble to the pack's doorstep, and I wouldn't blame him for tossing me off his land. For all I knew, the burrow might be bombarding him with threats in an effort to force my return.

I'd never heard of a female escaping the burrow who managed to evade the council permanently. The few who tried were dragged back so the leaders could use them as an example of what would happen if anyone else tried to leave.

As though the council could somehow see me, I shivered, feeling naked and exposed. Pushing to my feet, I found my raggedy, oversized shirt. I'd hoped the guys hadn't noticed the trembling of my hands, but as I slipped the shirt over my head, I found Fletcher's gold eyes watching me.

"Come here, love." He opened his arms.

I accepted his offer, sighing in relief as he wrapped me in a protective embrace.

Tucking my head under his chin, he whispered, "No matter what the future holds, you aren't alone. Remember that."

Fletcher didn't offer me pretty promises or assurances that nothing bad would ever happen. He offered me something more precious, a truth I could cling to.

"He's right," Copeland agreed, crossing his arms over his chest as though daring anyone to argue.

Linc's dark chuckle caused the three of us to turn and stare at him. "And if they somehow take us out, we'll drag an army of them down into Hades with us."

I hadn't expected such honesty. Caught off guard, a laugh escaped my lips. How could he be so playful and scary at the same time?

"Maybe it would be better to assure our mate we won't let anything happen to her?" Copeland snapped, unamused. "Violence isn't going to make her feel better, idiot!"

Linc shrugged. "I'm just letting her know if the worst-case scenario happens, we'll hurt more of them than they hurt of us. We have her back in life, or death, if it comes to it."

Copeland pinched the bridge of his nose. "There's something wrong with you."

"Probably." Linc smirked as he met my gaze. "I'm just the right amount of wrong, and I think our mate likes it."

My heart fluttered at the glint in his eyes that told me of all the wicked things he wanted to do with me. It was at that moment I realized I was into bad boys.

While I'd known I was in love with Fletcher for years, I'd never considered what other types of men I'd want in my fluffle. Why bother when you knew choosing who would be your mates was a dream you couldn't have?

I never would have guessed it, but I couldn't deny I was drawn like a dung beetle to elephant crap when it came to Linc. Something about his rough edges and bluntness made me feel safe.

And he was right. I relished knowing that if the council took me down, they'd do it at the cost of their own lives. Revenge was supposed to be beneath me, but I considered this more along the lines of returning a favor.

"Stop looking at her like that." Copeland waved a hand in front of Linc's face. "We need to stay focused and get packed up. No distractions!"

My inner bunny perked up her ears, knowing exactly what type of distractions he was talking about.

Fletcher cleared his throat. "Have you heard anything from the pack about the coyotes or our old burrow?"

"Yes, and what about the fire? Is it still burning?" I added, almost afraid to know the answer.

"The pack put out the fire and relocated everyone to a more protected area," Linc assured me. "Wolves are still stationed around the cave, although there weren't any disturbances overnight. The burrow hasn't reached out to anyone in the pack yet. As for the few coyotes who survived, they hightailed it off pack lands and disappeared."

"That's a relief." I let out the breath I hadn't realized I'd been holding. "How mad is the alpha that we brought trouble to his doorstep?"

"He's not mad at you," Copeland gave me a small smile. "You weren't hopping around starting fires or threatening the lives of his pack. The coyotes and your old burrow are the ones responsible, and they are the ones he's directing his fury toward. Stop trying to take the blame for things you had nothing to do with."

My laugh came out dry and brittle. "That's a lot easier said than done."

"Then we'll keep reminding you," Copeland teased gently. "We know it is stressful to move you during your heat, but even Monroe and the alpha feel we need to move from the cave to the house as soon as possible. The cave sits on the pack boundary, making it easier for them to attack."

"But where will we go?" I twisted the ends of my hair around my finger, unable to sit still thanks to the powerful combo of anxiety and hormones pumping through my veins.

"Home." Instead of his trademark smirk, Linc's smile was soft. "We're taking you home."

"I like the way that sounds." Smiling at the men, I fought the urge to pinch myself to make sure I wasn't dreaming.

Fletcher's muscles flexed, his arms tightening around me. "Just because Charlee is doing a little better and can go longer between breedings, doesn't mean it's safe to move her. The strain on her body could cause her to relapse and lose the progress we've made. Giving her body time to rest and recover is the most important thing right now."

Linc lifted an eyebrow, ready to challenge Fletcher. "You think we don't know that? Keeping our mate safe—and alive—is our top priority."

"Relax, you two. A fight will definitely stress our mate out." Copeland moved between the pair, using his bulky frame to block their line of sight. "Our house is deep inside pack land. It's surrounded by thick forests and deep ravines. The coyotes or burrow will have a hard time traversing that area if they decide to take another shot at kidnapping Charlee."

"How long will it take us to get to your house?" Fletcher asked, voice flat and unconvinced.

"From here?" Linc rubbed his jaw. "Three hours if we walk in our human forms. This cave is too remote to access with a vehicle, but we could walk to the nearest road and have a car meet us there. Even with a Jeep, it will take about two hours to get to the house. The road is unpaved and winds around the mountain, rather than being a straight shot. It's much quicker to make the trip in our wolf forms, which is how we usually get back and forth, other than a monthly supply run."

Fletcher narrowed his eyes, already having figured out where this was headed.

Copeland stepped in. "Listen, if you two shift to your rabbit forms and let us carry you, we can cover the distance in less than an hour."

My stomach churned. "I don't think that's such a good idea—"

Fletcher cut me off. "Done."

"Are you crazy? Why would you agree so readily?" I scrambled off his lap and stood, glaring at him. "You're seriously considering this?"

Fletcher calmly listened, then spoke. "If they were craving rabbit, they had ample opportunity to eat me yesterday. You trust them, right?"

"Of course I do! But that's not the—"

"Good. Since we both trust them, the decision is simple. Your body needs to rest, and the shorter the trip, the better. That is worth sacrificing my dignity for an hour."

I wanted to argue, but looking at Fletcher's bloodshot eyes and remembering the way he'd winced when moving around the cave made me swallow any further protests. He'd never admit that he wasn't up for the journey, but he needed rest just as much as I did. Especially after his desperate run the day before.

Turning away from the guys, I ran my fingers through

my hair and worked to steady my nerves. The plan made sense and would make things easier for all three of my mates, so I'd put on my metaphorical big girl panties and suck up any discomfort.

Linc appeared at my side, towering above me. "What do you need packed? You should rest while we take care of it. We'll just take the things that are valuable to you. I'll return later to do a full cleanup."

A snort escaped before I could stop it. "I have nothing."

Linc's eyes scanned the tiny confines of the cave as though sure he'd misheard me. "Nothing?"

"Monroe sent everything that's in here. Not even the shirt and pants are mine. Fletcher grabbed those from a metal giveaway drop-off bin in the last town before we got here."

"I'm sorry, sugar." Linc scooped me into his arms. "We'll make sure you get everything you deserve once you're settled in at home."

His cheek rubbed mine, the touch calming some of the anxiety that was searching for a foothold inside me.

"It's okay. I didn't really want to bring anything from the burrow. We keep things to remind us of good memories, and I have none from that place." Glancing at Fletcher over Linc's shoulder, I added, "There was only one thing there that brought me happiness, and I brought him with me."

"We won't forget him here then." Linc grinned at me. "Now, is there anything else you want to take with us?"

I took in the cave, pushing back the sadness at the

thought of leaving it. It was pathetic, but this was my nest, and leaving it was no easy feat. "The top blanket, please."

Copeland picked it up by the corner and wrinkled his nose. "It's covered in muddy wolf prints, sweat, and... other things. We have much softer blankets at the house. I promise."

Chewing my lip, I studied the blanket. Maybe they didn't want it dirtying their house.

"That's why she wants it." Fletcher took the blanket and folded it neatly. "Charlee started her heat without a nest, which is traumatic for a doe. Now we are making things worse by moving her before the heat is over. Having something from the original nest in the new one will help to calm her inner rabbit. It's a type of marking a space as yours, and she'll rest better surrounded by the scents."

"I didn't realize." Copeland bent and scooped all the bedding from the ground. "We'll take everything. The last thing we want is to make things harder on you."

Laughing, I wrapped my arms around his waist and hugged him. "Put those down. One blanket is enough. Besides, I prefer being surrounded by the three of you."

Copeland dropped the blankets and kissed the top of my head. "If you're sure?"

"I'm positive." Smiling up at him, I wondered not for the first time how I'd gotten so lucky.

"Good. Now let's get this show on the road." Linc scooped me up in his arms and headed out of the cave.

I blinked, my eyes struggling to adjust to the drastic

change in lighting from the dark cave to the brilliant morning sun.

Not wasting time, Fletcher stretched, then turned to Copeland. "Try not to drool all over me. Okay?"

Copeland rolled his eyes. "Wolves rule, we definitely don't drool."

Fletcher closed his eyes and let the change ripple over his body. His human form seemed to shimmer and wavered as the magic shifted him to the smaller rabbit form.

I'd never get tired of seeing him in this form. His glossy fur was white, but he had the cutest black muzzle, tall black ears, and black spots sprinkled down his side like fairy dust. He was beautiful.

Copeland squatted beside Fletcher. "I didn't get to tell you yesterday, but you are so adorable!" he cooed.

Fletcher gave a hard donkey kick to Copeland's shins, eliciting a hissing curse from the wolf shifter.

"Looks like we'd better stop underestimating rabbits." Linc threw back his head and laughed, while a gloating Fletcher sat back on his haunches.

"I see how it is," Copeland grumbled.

"Haven't you heard the old saying? If you don't have something nice to say, say nothing at all?" I scolded Copeland, doing my best to look serious, but struggling to hide my smile.

"But I was being nice," Copeland argued.

I snorted. "Uh-huh. Sure you were."

The boyish grin Copeland gave me just before he shifted was entirely unapologetic. The moment he was in wolf form, he lunged forward and scooped Fletcher up in his mouth. Ignoring the rabbit's angry grunts, the wolf darted into the forest, all the while his chest rumbled with the wolfy equivalent of laughter.

"He won't eat him, right?" I asked, needing the reassurance. "Fletcher looked so tiny in Copeland's jaws."

"Bunny Boy belongs to you, so he is under our protection." Linc followed that with a shrug, then added, "Besides, he didn't eat him yesterday, so I'd say he can resist temptation today too."

"Maybe you could come up with a nickname other than Bunny Boy?" Trusting my wolf mates, I turned away from the tree-line. "Your wolves are truly okay having a bunny as a mate? And being part of a fluffle that includes a male rabbit?"

These were questions I knew I should ask later. Time was running out before the next wave of my heat hit, but, unable to help myself, I continued stalling.

"Our wolves are getting used to the idea of sharing you, and our space, with a male shifter of another species. But our wolves wouldn't hurt him for one simple reason: it would upset you, and that's unacceptable. Copeland would die to protect your rabbit male, so stop worrying. The sooner we are out of the open, the happier I will be." He bent and laid the blanket on the ground. "Shift and sit in the middle. I'll pick up the corners and carry you back. It'll be more comfortable than being clamped between my jaws."

"Why didn't Copeland do that for Fletcher?" I asked, wondering why I hadn't thought of that sooner.

Linc chuckled. "Because he's having fun messing with Bunny Boy." He pulled me into his arms and nuzzled the top of my hair.

"You really need to come up with a different nickname before he smothers you in your sleep." Happy to delay shifting, I cuddled against him, pressing my cheek against his stomach.

Chapter EIGHT

LINC

I held Charlee against me. "Something is bothering you, and it has nothing to do with my creative nick-names," I teased, hoping to ease the tension radiating from her. "Is your heat stirring already?"

Charlee waved a hand dismissively. "My heat is tolerable."

I knew it was a lie. She wasn't as skilled at hiding her distress as she believed.

What she needed was a month of sleep and four-course meals to put weight back on her fragile body. Wasting energy on mating was the last thing she needed to be doing, yet it was the thing her heat relentlessly drove her to seek. I'd eagerly taken her up on sex every time she desired it, but I couldn't ignore the guilt in the pit of my stomach over how much I selfishly enjoyed it.

"If it's not the heat, then what's bothering you?" I ran

my hands down her back. "Until I know the problem, I can't fix it."

"It's not that simple. You can't fix everything, Linc." Her words were muffled against my chest.

I feigned a hiss of pain. "I'm hurt. We've been mates less than a week, and you're already doubting my abilities."

She huffed a soft laugh, but didn't enlighten me any further. I was left trying to puzzle it out on my own.

She was fine until we'd talked about making the move to the house…

"Are you sure there isn't anything else you need from the cave? I don't mind carrying the extra weight."

Charlee shook her head. "I'm sure."

"If it's not something you want from the cave, are you worried about the house? Copeland and I have never had a woman there, other than Monroe when she visited with the alpha."

Sighing, she pushed away from me. "I'm not worried about the house or stuff. Let's just get this over with."

She doesn't want to shift.

Forcing her to look at me, I studied her expression. "Are you afraid I'll hurt you if you shift? I swear you're safe with me."

Her eyes widened with surprise. "Of course not! It's actually unbelievable that you're a stranger, but I'm already so comfortable with you."

My relief quickly morphed into confusion. If she wasn't afraid, then why the reluctance?

The truth dawned on me. "You hate feeling vulnerable."

Her bottom lip quivered. "Shifting is something I avoid as much as possible. I stay in my human form because I wouldn't have survived most of what I've gone through if I'd been in such a weak form."

Dropping her head, she stared at the ground. "When we escaped, we stayed in our rabbit forms for nearly two weeks. It was mentally taxing. I'd hoped to avoid it, at least for a while, because it stirs up a lot of memories for me—none of them good."

My heart ached for my broken mate. Shifters relished their abilities, yet she almost despised that part of herself. It made me seethe with rage at everyone in her burrow who'd caused this trauma.

I longed for the time when she'd open up and trust us with the secrets of her past. When her heat was over, I'd make sure she was given a safe space to heal and learn to love both sides of herself. But this wasn't the time to push it.

"I can shift and let you climb on my back. That way, you won't have to shift. My wolf can easily carry you back to the house," I offered, wanting her to be comfortable.

"Thank you, but no." Charlee grabbed the hem of her shirt to pull it over her head. "I can shift, so there is no reason to make the journey harder on you."

Chapter
NINE

CHARLEE

I wish I could say I remembered the trip to the cabin. But my fatigue, and the gentle rocking caused by the wolf's long, loping stride, lulled me to sleep.

Barking in the distance roused me from my nap. With a yawn, I poked my head out of the makeshift rucksack and blinked at my surroundings.

The guys hadn't described their home, but for some reason, I'd imagined they lived in a small hunter's cabin. That couldn't have been further from the truth. As Linc ran up the long trail leading to the house, I took in the sprawling, red brick Château. It looked like it belonged in the French countryside, back in a time when the wealthy enjoyed bragging about having a city home and a country estate.

Thick evergreen pines pressed in on all sides of the

house. Several large oak trees stood among them, their expansive canopies blocking out most of the sun. Ivy crept over the bricks, covering the outside walls, as though trying to reclaim the land for Mother Nature.

If it hadn't been for the wolf sitting on the porch, his tail wagging and tongue lolling out of his mouth in a toothy smile, the scene would have been depressing. It was clearly well kept, but somehow, it also seemed desolate. A tragic piece of some forgotten paradise.

"It's about time you guys got here! Copeland refuses to shift," Fletcher grumbled from where he sat on the front porch stairs. "I swear! If he licks me one more time, or brings that stupid stick for me to toss again, I'm going to lose my mind."

My nose twitched, and I was thankful not to be in my human form. Fletcher probably wouldn't have appreciated my amusement.

"Do they know that they're men? Or do they just go into full dog mode when they shift?" Fletcher asked, picking up the stick and tossing it onto the patch of grass in front of the house.

With a gleeful bark, Copeland dashed off the porch to relieve it.

"When we're in our rabbit form, we're still very much human in our brains. But it's like there's nothing but a 'good boi' in this guy's head."

At the words 'good boi,' Copeland scrambled back up the porch steps and dropped the extra slobbery stick into Fletcher's lap.

I wasn't an expert on wolf shifters, but I suspected Copeland was simply messing with Fletcher. Linc's amused, wolfish chuff further confirmed my suspicions.

When we reached the foot of the stairs, Linc lowered his head and set the blanket on the ground. Unclasping his jaw, he released the fabric, letting it fall around me. With a yawn, I stretched my front paws out in front of me and arched my back, trying to ease the muscle cramps from staying still for so long.

One minute, I was doing the bunny version of Downward Dog. And the next, I found myself flying toward the sky, no longer bound by the laws of gravity.

"You're the most adorable thing I've ever seen!" Copeland held me level with his face.

I rolled my eyes and grunted at his ridiculousness.

Fletcher laughed. "If you keep that up, Charlee is going to kick the shifter out of you."

Ignoring the warning, Copeland flipped me on my back, cradling me against his chest as though holding a newborn baby. "Who's the cutest bunny in the world? You are!" He continued cooing absolute nonsense.

I kicked out with my hind legs, trying to shove his hand away from tickling my stomach. Some people could see an adorable animal and keep walking, remaining unaffected. Copeland definitely wasn't one of them.

"If I were you, I'd sleep with one eye open tonight." Fletcher tried, but failed to hide his amusement.

"She couldn't kill me if she tried. Look at her! She's so

small!" Copeland ducked his head, rubbing his nose against mine.

"Don't say I didn't warn you. She has a bit of a reputation. One that she earned." Fletcher didn't bother to hide the pride in his voice.

"Is that so?" Copeland scratched under my chin while I did my best to pretend I didn't like it. "Are you my Wee Warrior?"

Hellebores! He did not just go there...

Without warning, or thinking about how far off the ground I was, I shifted. Copeland's eyes widened, but to his credit, he didn't drop me.

"You can call me Tiny Titan, Fun-sized Fury, Petite Powerhouse, even The Micro Avenger." I glared up at him. "But if you ever call me Wee Warrior again, it won't be the little pig crying *wee-wee-wee* all the way home—it will be you, Wolf!"

Linc must have shifted while I was distracted because his and Fletcher's howls of laughter were very human.

"Yes, ma'am." Copeland bit the inside of his cheeks, already knowing better than to let me see a smirk.

"Now, put me down," I ordered.

Copeland obediently set me on my feet and stared down at me, his face turning red as he held in his laughter.

I narrowed my eyes in warning. "If you so much as giggle..."

"Wouldn't dream of it," he replied innocently.

Crossing my arms over my chest, I was suddenly reminded I was still rocking my birthday suit. It didn't matter that they'd seen every inch of my skin; I couldn't stop my full-body flush. Being naked during sex was one thing. Prancing around naked with three men watching was something that would take some getting used to.

I spun around, snatching the blanket from the ground, intending to wrap it around me. Linc caught my wrist.

"Sugar, you have no reason to feel shy. You're a work of art." He brushed his lips against the inside of my wrist. "But if you would feel more comfortable clothed, then let's go inside and get you a clean shirt." Linc moved his palm against my lower back, guiding me up the porch steps and into the house.

"I think we'd all enjoy some food and a long shower," Copeland agreed. "Come on, Fletch."

We let the wolves lead us into the kitchen. While the outside of the house looked as though it had belonged in a long-forgotten fairytale, the interior was more in line with our current century. The guys had updated the furniture, light fixtures and appliances, but had managed to keep some of the homey rustic feel.

Stepping to a cabinet that stood just inside the home's entrance, Copeland pulled out three pairs of folded gym shorts. He tossed a pair to Fletcher and then Linc before slipping a pair on himself.

My stomach flipped as he pulled two more folded garments from the shelf. Even though Linc had assured me no female had stayed in their home, part of my soul shriveled up and died just thinking that he was about to offer me clothes that were from an ex.

He stared down at the shorts and T-shirt in his hand. "No matter how tight you draw the string, I don't think our shorts are going to fit you very well."

Grinning in relief, I caught his face between my palms, pulling him down so I could kiss his cheek. "The shirt will be fine."

I slipped it on, unsurprised when it fell past my knees. Spinning in a circle as though I were the belle of the ball, I giggled, "It's practically a dress on me."

"And it looks beautiful." Copeland brushed his thumb along my cheekbone. "Once your heat is over, I swear we'll take you to get whatever you need."

"Unless you prefer to make a list. The women from the pack would be happy to bring you whatever you need now," Linc offered.

"No!" It came out a bit too sharp, and I forced a smile to my lips to make up for it. "I don't really need anything right now. All we've been doing is eating and sleeping."

"Just know the offer is there should you change your mind." Linc moved past me, toward the largest fireplace I'd ever seen.

It stood in the middle of the floor, serving as a dividing wall between the kitchen and the main room. My eyes slid around the room, suddenly suspicious.

"Did you buy this house from a witch who enjoyed combining her love of DIY projects and gingerbread baking? The same witch who liked cookouts involving kids? And I don't mean the goat kind of kids..." I asked.

"I was wondering what the initials 'H & G' carved in the

basement meant," Copeland teased—or at least I hoped he was teasing.

Before I could do something stupid, like lick the wall nearest me to make sure it was made of wood and not a twisted dessert, Copeland swept me up into his arms. Striding across the room, he deposited me in the middle of a bean bag the size of a bed... where I promptly disappeared.

I squirmed, trying to free myself, only to be swallowed even deeper.

"Do you want help?" Copeland asked, brow raised as he watched the battle playing out in front of him.

"No!" Flinging out my limbs like a spider, I tried to distribute my weight evenly to keep from sinking through all seven levels of bean bag hell. "I totally have this under control."

"Uh-huh. Sure you do." Fletcher sat down on the couch across from the bag and laced his fingers behind his head to enjoy the show.

Ignoring both men, I gathered my strength, preparing to fling myself from the cursed cushion masquerading as a chair. The moment my weight shifted, the seat devoured me faster than a hungry hippo.

"Ugh! I thought you said I was going to eat! You said nothing about me getting eaten!"

"That was an oversight on his part. You're definitely going to get eaten." Glancing toward the fireplace, I caught Linc's smirk and the wicked gleam in his eyes. "Over and over."

My entire body flushed at the implication, and I gave myself over to the beanbag, willingly allowing it to swallow me so I could hide—not from embarrassment over his words, but to keep them from seeing just how badly I wanted them.

My reprieve was short-lived. A hand reached into the depths and pulled me from the belly of the bag.

"You're so tiny, we'll have to be careful not to lose you." Copeland grinned down at me. "How do you feel about wearing one of those kid leashes?"

I wrinkled my nose in disgust. "How do you feel about having me shove a glowstick up your dick and cracking it?"

"If it means having your hands on me, I don't mind." Copeland headed toward the kitchen. "I'm going to make us some food before I decide to take you up on that offer."

I gaped at his retreating back.

And this is why you're supposed to date people before marrying them, Charlee. You have to give them time to slip and let their crazy show.

I tried not to wonder about what other things he might have been into in the bedroom.

Don't panic. As long as it doesn't involve leaving cookie crumbs in the bed, I can handle it. Probably, I mentally assured myself.

COPELAND DIPPED a spoon into the bowl of soup and held it to my lips. "Open wide."

"That's what she said," I snickered, but obediently parted my lips.

As the warm broth hit my stomach, I was reminded of how long it had been since I'd eaten regular meals. We'd had the food in the cave, but that was very different from a home-cooked meal. I fought the intrusive thoughts that wanted me to snatch the cup from his hand and guzzle it down in a few big gulps.

Copeland noticed my struggle and lifted the bowl to my lips so I could take bigger sips. "There's no rush. Once we make sure the soup broth settles your stomach and doesn't make you sick, I'll make you a plate of real food."

"I should have gotten you out of there sooner." Fletcher let out a string of curses. "And I shouldn't have pushed us so hard to get here. If we'd stopped to rest more, you wouldn't be starved and exhausted."

Swallowing the liquid in my mouth, I leaned toward him and caught his hand. "If we'd slowed down, we might not have made it before their hired coyotes. We made it. That's all thanks to you." I squeezed his hand, hoping to reassure him, but Fletcher wasn't having it.

Pulling his hand from mine, he grabbed my chin. His grip was firm, but not painful as he forced me to look him in the eyes. The self-loathing and pain I saw swirling in those golden depths shattered my heart.

"We both know it was the stress of the journey and the toll it took on your body that sent you into heat early!

You've practically had a feral heat—and don't even try to deny it!" he added the last bit, seeing I was about to protest. "If the wolves hadn't shown up when they did, you'd still be in pain—if you were conscious at all. There's only so much one mate can do!"

"But they did show up." I brushed my hand along his cheek. "It all worked out. We're safe and we get to stay together."

"You don't get it, Charlee!" Fletcher's breathing was ragged, forcing him to pause between words. "I wanted to save you, but I very nearly killed you!" His eyes glittered with angry tears, shocking me more than his sudden outburst.

In all my years at the burrow, I'd never seen a male rabbit shed so much as a single tear. Not even when losing a loved one. Too stunned to speak, I could do nothing but press my palm against his cheek, hoping to comfort him.

"I took you from the burrow, so you'd have a choice in who you bonded with. Only to see you bonded to two wolves you don't even know!" Fletcher shot a quick look at the wolves. "No offense."

Linc shrugged. "None taken."

They might not have been offended, but I was.

"Stop this right now!" I pulled my face free of his grip, straightened my posture, and glared at him. "You and I both know this is infinitely better than the situation I was in! The two aren't even comparable!"

"Either way, you are being forced to spend your first heat with strangers!" Fletcher argued.

"I bonded with two men who pledged to protect me and my heart. I've been snuggled, cared for, and fed by my fluffle during this heat." Blood pounded in my ears as fury took control. "Have you forgotten what awaited me on my first heat in the burrow?"

The muscle in Fletcher's jaw flexed, and his eyes darkened with barely suppressed rage. He hadn't forgotten.

But I was angry and couldn't stop myself from reminding him. "The burrow can frame it however they want, but we both know the truth. The moment I went into heat, I would have been given a room in the bunny brothel. The burrow can claim that the building was created to give the women a community and keep them safe, but it's a lie. They built it to keep us like pets for their entertainment and pleasure."

My chest tightened with each sentence, making it harder to draw in a breath, but I wasn't finished. "I would've had no say in which men from the burrow bought, won, or earned the right to come into my room. The council knows that my rabbit would have formed a mate bond with each of those men—men who don't care about anything other than getting their rocks off with the newest piece of cottontail. No one cared. Why would they?"

The sharp spike in my temperature had nothing to do with my anger. A powerful cramp twisted my insides, nearly sending me to my knees. I continued to ignore the demands of the heat that were growing stronger, because having Fletcher understand me was something I needed more.

"The more men my stupid little heart bonded to, the more control the burrow would have over me, since I'd never be able to leave unless I was willing to risk dying from separation." My hands balled into fists at my sides. "I never would have had a fluffle of my own. And for the first time in my life, I feel loved!"

Chapter TEN

LINC

"They planned to do what?"

Charlee must've forgotten Copeland and I were still in the room, witnessing the outburst, because my roar of outrage caused her to jump, her trembling hand clutching the front of the T-shirt over her heart.

"Linc!" Copeland snapped, leaping up to wrap her protectively in his arms.

I hadn't meant to scare her, but my wolf was rattling its cage, making it impossible to think with clarity.

"What was your burrow planning for you?" I repeated my question, doing my best to rein in my rage.

"Our burrow takes the stance that the females belong to all the men. They claim it's a way to ensure every woman receives equal attention and has all her needs met. But that's a pretty lie to cover up the truth," Charlee answered, her words slow and measured.

I heard the words, but couldn't seem to process them. "What about having a home? A family?"

Charlee refused to lift her gaze from the floor. "Women don't get to have possessions. The men own all the land and houses, while the women live together in a community building with individual rooms. Like a dorm room. The only time we stay somewhere else is if a fluffle takes you to their home for a few days."

"The men in your burrow can check females out like they're library books to enjoy and then return when they're ready for the next one?" I prayed I had misunderstood.

It was Fletcher who answered this time. "Pretty much. The only women off limits are those who are pregnant and those who haven't had their first heat. But once a female has her first heat, she's considered fair game."

"What about pregnant females? Do their mates take care of them?" Copeland asked.

Charlee scoffed. "Are you joking? That would require too much work for the men. Pregnant women stay in the community building and are cared for by the other females. The only reason we know who our fathers are is from the paternity test done at birth. The test isn't done so that the male can step up and be a dad—" She gave a harsh laugh before continuing. "No, it's just to make sure no inbreeding happens. The only time I met my father was when I passed him in the hallway when he was on the way to a booty call."

I couldn't have spoken if I'd wanted to. The hair on my arms stood on end as my wolf's magic pushed to the surface, trying to force a shift. Not yet. I needed to learn as much as I could about the men I'd be taking off the Grim Reaper's roster ASAP.

"And the children?" Copeland rubbed slow, soothing circles on her lower back.

Charlee stared unseeing out the window. "They are raised by the women until they reach school age. Then they're moved to a part of the building that is dedicated to them. The women take turns volunteering, so you still see your kids, but they are raised by the community."

Copeland's hand froze. "The dads aren't involved at all?"

"Not with the girls. Once a boy is older, a lot of the dads will start spending time with them and preparing them for their place in the burrow." Charlee sighed. "It wasn't all bad. As long as we didn't question the men, we were treated well."

"How can you say that?!" Fletcher dropped his hands, staring at her in disbelief.

Charlee shrugged. "Most of the women were satisfied with how things were done. I was told countless times to stop complaining because we were well fed, clothed, and safe."

"They are probably brainwashed!" I growled. "None of this is normal or anywhere close to being acceptable."

Fletcher strode across the room and kneeled in front of her. "Charlee, you didn't deserve any of the punishments the council poured out on you."

Her lip trembled as she continued staring out the

window. "If I'd stayed quiet, I wouldn't have kept being tossed in front of the council for breaking the rules."

"You were imprisoned for three weeks for asking to choose your mates. You were starved for building a tree-house to hide away from the noise of the dorms. You were beaten until you couldn't walk because you went to the lake to swim instead of attending the burrow's party where they show off the women about to go into heat as if you were all part of a meat market. You were stripped naked and caged in the middle of the town for demanding the right to decide who shared your bed." Fletcher's chest was heaving by the time he finished.

Reaching out, he gently lifted the hem of the shirt, displaying the pale white lines. Charlee shivered as he brushed his fingers across them.

"How many times? How many times were you whipped for no other reason than asking them to explain their reasoning? For daring to question them? For pleading for rights that were unquestionably yours?" A tear slid down the male rabbit's cheek, but I felt no pity.

The only thing I wanted to feel was my fingers around his neck, strangling the life out of him.

"You were always there for me." Charlee turned and rested her hand on his cheek. "Sneaking me food, cleaning my wounds, sleeping outside the cage. Remember when the council discovered you'd given me your coat to cover myself with inside the cage? They forced me to give it back because I wasn't allowed to wear any garment as part of the punishment."

Charlee laughed. "So you covered the entire cage with blankets, and when they demanded you remove them, you told them I wasn't wearing anything, only the cage was. They were livid! I thought your dad was going to throw you inside the cage with me."

Fletcher gave her a fleeting smile, then grew serious. "I should have found ways to protect you better from my father and the rest of the council."

"How many beatings did you get because of me? And yet you still slept beside the cage every night, even though you knew you'd be punished the following morning." Charlee's eyes sparkled with unshed tears. "Do you think I didn't notice when you wore long sleeves on hot days to hide the bruises? Or how you'd try to hide your pain from me when you walked? You are a shifter; your body would have healed superficial injuries. Which could only mean you were being dealt vicious injuries because of me."

I tried to be patient while they had their moment, but I could no longer hold my tongue. "Your father is a councilman?"

"Yes. My father is on the council, and the burrow planned for me to take his position when he retired."

"So you were in a position of power and allowed them to torture Charlee?" I gripped the arms of my chair, trying to keep myself from attacking him.

Rage flared in Fletcher's eyes. "Of course not!" His spark of anger died as quickly as it had appeared. "The only reason I went along with the training was to find a way to change things. I wanted to be a voice of reason and optimistically believed others would want change as well. Turns out, I was wrong."

"At least you tried." Charlee leaned forward and kissed his cheek.

Fletcher shook his head in disgust. "I wanted things to be better for you and all the other women. It nearly killed me when I realized it would be impossible to get enough of the council on my side to vote in change."

"They kicked you out?" Copeland asked, his tone sharp. "Is that why you helped Charlee escape? Because it was the only way you'd get to have her?"

A muscle in Fletcher's jaw ticked, and he took his time before answering. "I helped Charlee escape because her heat was coming. If they weren't able to break her will and get her to conform to the burrow's ways before then, they'd decided she was to be silenced."

The statement hit me like a physical blow. They were going to kill her because they couldn't control her.

Kill. Kill. Kill.

"Besides, I didn't have to leave to have her." Fletcher's words were so soft I barely heard them over the battle chant echoing in my mind. He met her eyes, then looked away. "The council offered to give you to me if I would fall in line and stop stirring up headaches during council meetings."

"I'm not surprised. Women are nothing more than pawns. But why didn't you tell me?" Her voice shook. "I was so caught up in my fears and life struggles. You always listened and comforted me, but you never told me what you were going through. I can't imagine how hard it must've been to go against the expectations of your father and the council."

"Because you had enough to deal with. I didn't want to add to your pain." Fletcher tried to pull her from Copeland's lap, but stopped when the wolf growled. Giving up, he caught her face between his hands and gently kissed her. "And I was too ashamed to admit I'd failed you."

"You didn't fail me," Charlee rushed to assure him. "But why didn't you accept their offer? You said you'd been in love with me long before we ran, so why not accept their offer?"

"Because you deserved more than that. Because I couldn't let you stay around them for another day." Fletcher's shoulders sagged as though he were carrying the weight of the world on them, or perhaps just the weight of his memories and guilt.

Some of my anger eased. Okay, I wouldn't kill him, just maim him a little.

"The council had to know one male wouldn't have gotten her through her heat, so how was that offer going to work?" Copeland asked.

"In exchange for me accepting our customs and stopping fighting against the will of the council, they'd let me keep Charlee in my home—as long as I kept her under control and away from the other women who might be influenced by her 'unbecoming' behavior." Fletcher's lip curled in disgust as he said the last. "During her heat, she'd be available to the other men, but outside of her heat, none of them would be allowed to touch her."

"How generous," I snarled, shoving to my feet and beginning to pace.

"Sadly, for the burrow, that was beyond generous—especially considering how little they thought of me." Charlee seemed unfazed by her burrow's latest atrocity. "For them to make this offer, it shows how much they respected, or feared, Fletcher's influence."

"It was their way of controlling both of us," said Fletcher. "My father didn't want to face the embarrassment of having his heir removed from future leadership. And since they couldn't let me leave the burrow for fear of my telling the world how they were running things, I'd become a problem. You were the carrot they dangled in front of me in hopes of solving both their problems at once."

"Why didn't you tell me?" Charlee chewed her lip, trying to figure out why he'd hidden it.

"I'd like to know the answer to that as well." Copeland's voice was void of any emotion, and he watched Fletcher with the steady gaze of a predator on the prowl.

If he lost control and injured the male rabbit, it would break Charlee's heart. I also knew I'd be unable to stop him, not when my bloodlust was simmering just under the surface.

"Because I knew you were tired and your body was giving out from the constant beatings. I was afraid you would agree to those terms because it was a slight improvement to the alternative." Fletcher stared down at the floor. "And I knew I couldn't stand by while they continued treating the rest of the women the same as they always had.

But if I didn't keep my mouth shut, they'd take you from me and punish you to keep me in line."

"Oh, Fletcher!" Charlee sobbed, wrenching herself free from Copeland and throwing herself into Fletcher's arms.

He crushed her against his chest. "And because I never wanted you to believe you were something that could be given and taken at their whim, as though you were nothing more than property on loan."

Charlee's sniffles shredded my soul. She'd gone through so much, and I was in awe of how much strength was packed into such a tiny body.

Fletcher gently rocked her, trying to comfort her. "Besides, their offer was empty because I didn't just want your body. The only one who could give me what I wanted was you because I wanted your heart... but only if you gave it to me freely."

The fury I'd felt toward Fletcher vanished. He'd been young and still had done everything he could to protect her. And then, instead of taking the prize they'd offered, he'd risked everything to give her a chance at a life outside the burrow. A chance at freedom.

"I respect you for going against everything you were raised to believe in. That isn't easy." I paused to clear my throat. "And I will forever be thankful that you did. You brought my mate to our doorstep. You're not so bad, Rabbit."

"Same to you, Wolf." Fletcher gave me a nod. "You need to let the alpha know the council has hired coyotes as enforcers to collect debts. Our burrow has made a fortune offering high-interest loans to people down on their luck."

"That is predatory, which is weird, coming from a shifter species that's supposed to be prey," Copeland pointed out.

"So the burrow may have hired the coyotes to what? Find you two? Kidnap Charlee?" I asked.

"Most likely, they have orders to bring Charlee back. The council knows if they get to her, I'd return to the burrow as well." Fletcher paused, then added, "It's also possible they have an order to kill us before we have a chance to tell our story and stir up trouble for them."

They wanted to drag my mate back to the burrow to be used by other men? And if that failed, they were going to kill her?

I'd die before I let them so much as breathe in her direction. My wolf was rabid with the need to seek vengeance, but I needed a plan before I released him.

Hunt them down.

Kill them.

Find a sorcerer.

Bring them back from the grave.

Kill them again.

Rinse and repeat.

Yeah. That would work for me.

With a plan in place, I stood from the fireplace hearth and headed for the door.

"Where are you going?" Copeland asked.

"To commit mass murder." Realizing my mate might

think I was upset with her, I softened my tone and added, "I'll bring muffins when I come back."

Rustling came from behind me, but I would not be stopped. Not by anything.

"You can't go fight an entire burrow on your own! After our mate's heat is over, we'll go together." Copeland said, appearing at my side. "Besides, you'd be a total dick if you hogged all the bloodshed for yourself."

Copeland's words reminded me of why he was my best friend. He knew my plan was risky, but he also recognized that he couldn't talk me out of something once I'd made up my mind. And he was willing to charge into danger by my side.

"Fine. I won't visit the burrow until her heat is over. But my wolf needs to run." Not waiting for a response, I took off toward the thick tree-line.

I didn't even slow as the magic of the shift rippled over my skin and my paws thundered over the forest floor. Hopefully, the run would burn off some of the violent energy that threatened to consume me.

Chapter ELEVEN

LINC

Two hours later, I pushed open the door and padded into the house. Not wanting to wake anyone if they were sleeping, I kept my steps soft, my paws not making a sound against the hardwood. Tilting back my head, I sniffed, letting the array of scents paint a picture of what had happened since I'd left.

Salty tears and sweat. The aroma of the soup and bread-sticks Copeland had prepared for dinner hours before. The dessert-like scent of her heat, the earthy scent of sex.

It was that last fragrance that caused my wolf's most primal instincts to flare. He was less than pleased at the idea of another male touching our mate. I sympathized, but sharing was something I could live with as long as I got to call Charlee mine.

Besides, she'd let me mark her in the cave, and now she bore the imprint of my bite. I'd been hyped up on the fight and adrenaline from my injuries when I padded into the cave and found her drenched in the scent of her heat. Even though her inner rabbit must have been telling her to run from the fray and from my bloody wolf form, she'd trusted me to bite her and not lose control. My mate was tough.

Heading down the hall, I pushed open my bedroom door to find the furniture had been shoved against the wall. It looked like they'd gathered every mattress in the house and put them on the floor to create one giant bed. I made a mental note to start working on a custom bedframe once she was safely through her heat.

The mattresses were piled high with a dozen pillows, and I could see at least four blankets. Moving closer, I found Charlee curled up on her side between the two men. I'd marked the right side of her neck, and now I could see the imprint of Copeland's mate mark on the left side; he'd claimed her as well.

My wolf was significantly larger than that of a natural wolf, which was why I wasn't part of the team that handled perimeter security. If a hunter spotted me, the humans would be crawling all over our land within days.

Yep. I could see the headlines now: *Beast of Gévaudan Returns from the Grave to Haunt American Forest.*

Letting my jealousy get the best of me, I used the bulk and size of my wolf's form to shove a complaining Copeland out of the way. I squeezed between them, dropping to my belly beside Charlee.

For the thousandth time, I was stunned by how fragile she seemed. The other two rabbit shifter females were about the same height, but Monroe's fiery stubbornness had made her seem taller. I knew Charlee must have that same spirit and resilience to survive what she'd gone through, but at that moment, it looked like a summer breeze could knock her down.

What if I accidentally rolled over and squished her in our sleep? My huff of worry caused her eyelids to fly open. She took in my wolf form and her eyes widened.

The first time we'd met, I'd been in my wolf form, but she had been caught in the throes of her heat and mid-bonding with Fletcher. She'd happily curled her fingers into my fur, using me as an anchor to keep from going wild on the male rabbit. The second time she'd encountered my wolf had been when we'd pinned her beneath us, spurred on by her frenzied heat.

We were mates, but that didn't change the fact that to be comfortable with me, she'd need to ignore centuries of a prey species' survival instincts telling her I was dangerous. I held myself motionless, waiting for her reaction and steeling myself against the pain I'd experience if she recoiled in fear or disgust—even if the reaction was automatic.

"Hello." Her voice was husky thanks to sleep... and sex.

I tilted my head in greeting, not wanting to startle her with any sudden movements. Charlee held her hand near my muzzle as though I were a dog, and she was waiting for me to sniff it and accept her touch.

My wolf rolled his eyes. Little Miss Bunny Britches had a lot to learn about wolves. Leaning forward, I pressed my nose against her palm and was amazed when it nearly took up her entire palm.

Charlee sucked in her breath and gave me a brilliant smile. "Can I pet you?"

Pet me? Was she serious? My chuff caused tendrils of blonde hair to blow around her face. As if I would lower myself—

My wolf flopped onto his back, presenting our stomach for belly rubs.

Mate wants to pet.

I was surprised because my wolf rarely spoke. My disgruntled attitude evaporated the instant she ran her fingers through my underbelly fur.

"I've never felt anything this soft," she whispered in awe.

Soft wasn't a compliment most men wanted to hear, but I wasn't going to complain. Who knew belly rubs felt so good?

Charlee laughed as my wolf gave a happy wiggle. She scratched my stomach with more enthusiasm, stretching as far as she could reach. With a well-timed bump of my hips, I knocked her off balance and caused her to face-plant against my fur. Not giving her time to recover, I wedged my nuzzle under her butt and, with a firm jerk, tossed her onto my stomach.

"Umpf!" Her grunt of surprise was followed by a squeal as I snuck a quick lick up her cheek.

"I see how it is!" She ran her hands through my fur with renewed fervor, as though she were trying to tickle me.

Copeland clicked his tongue in disbelief. "Oh, how the mighty have fallen."

"Why would you say that?" Charlee pushed herself onto her knees, straddling my chest, and narrowed her eyes in his direction.

"Wolves don't present their stomachs to other shifters, and wolf shifters don't degrade themselves by being petted," he explained.

Charlee scoffed. "But he likes it! See?" Her hands scratched at my ribs.

I could totally play this cool—

My wolf let my tongue loll out of my mouth and kicked at the air with our back leg as she found *the* spot.

Yeah, that was exactly what I'd meant by playing it cool.

You whine more than a dog.

This was the most talkative my wolf had ever been. Go figure it would be to insult me.

"From werewolf to purse pet." Copeland's dark chuckle told me I wouldn't live this down for a long time.

"Stop being mean," Charlee scolded, adding a little growl.

Since when did she growl?

Mate so cute. My wolf practically gushed.

Hades! What was going on? My bunny mate was snarling like a pup, and my wolf was about a minute away from offering to make friendship bracelets with her.

Copeland continued to laugh, but Charlee wasn't having it. "I bet you'd like being petted too!"

"Little rabbit, there isn't a chance that's going to happen." He shook his head.

Charlee slid off me and stood. "I'd like you to shift. Now."

Copeland raised an eyebrow. "Sugar, you can't be serious."

"The hare I am!" Crossing her arms over her chest, she pinned him with a stern glare. "Shift. Please."

Copeland threw back his head and laughed. "Little mate, my wolf will never degrade himself like that."

My wolf thumped his tail against the floor, thoroughly delighted at our mate's bossiness.

"Should we do something?" Fletcher whispered, his gaze darting between the pair locked in a stare down.

If I'd been in my human form, I would've suggested making popcorn.

The silence stretched until Copeland threw up his hands. "Fine, but only because you said please."

"Thank you!" Charlee beamed at him.

My best friend shifted. It took him longer than me to complete, but it was far smoother than most of the packs' shifting ability.

"Good boy. Now roll over," Charlee ordered.

Surely she hadn't just called him a good boy? Belly rubs were one thing. Being a good boy was another.

My wolf rumbled with wicked delight while Copeland snarled in displeasure.

Instead of backing down, our petite princess lifted her

chin. "You are welcome to complain about it, but I want you to roll over."

Copeland stalked toward her, closing the gap between them in seconds. He stared stubbornly at her with glowing gold eyes.

I thought she'd back down. Her inner beast had to be begging her to run. Instead, she stepped forward so that the pair were nearly touching noses. Other than the slight hitch in her breathing, she showed no sign of fear while facing off with a predator.

"Charlee, maybe it's best you don't antagonize him." Fletcher caught her hand, trying to tug her away from the glowering wolf.

I didn't blame him. Copeland could be goofy one minute and intimidating the next. He wasn't an alpha, but his confident swagger definitely gave off powerful vibes—something he enjoyed flexing. I was several years older than him, but because of being less outgoing, I blended into the shadows while he drew the attention. Even now, the rabbit shifter had his back turned to me while focusing his full attention on Copeland, wrongly assuming I was less of a threat.

"Linc?" Charlee glanced over her shoulder at me, then pointed at Copeland. "Pin him for me."

My wolf chortled in glee.

Our mate knew who held the real power here.

Copeland didn't stand a chance.

My muscles tightened as I sprang forward, taking the wolf down in a single smooth move. His back collided with the hardwood floor. Locking my jaws around his throat, I dug my razor-sharp canines into his skin, warning him of the consequences of fighting against me.

"Thank you, handsome." Charlee kissed the top of my head, then bent to stare Copeland in the eyes. "We're still getting to know each other, but I need to be clear about something."

Keeping him pinned, I watched from the corner of my eye as she dropped to her knees.

"I enjoy teasing, but never when it is over a moment of intimacy with my mates. How can we be vulnerable with each other if we have to worry about being judged?" She practically purred each word in his ear.

When her fingers teased across the creamy fur of Copeland's stomach, his chest rumbled with a sound of pure delight. It took everything in me to keep from drawing blood over his idiotic behavior. He'd made such a big deal out of a belly rub and then had the audacity to melt at the first touch of her hand? Or was my irritation because it wasn't my stomach getting petted?

Releasing his neck, I sat back and watched.

"See? It's not so bad, huh?" She scratched more enthusiastically.

Copeland's tail swished the floor like he was a freaking golden retriever instead of a wolf. Charlee laughed and went to place a kiss on his belly, only to gasp when he shifted back to his human form and her lips pressed against his abs.

"Just so you know, I never minded having you pet me."

Wrapping an arm around her waist, he pulled Charlee down on top of him. "I'm down for having you rub my belly—or anywhere else—whenever you want."

Her eyebrows drew together. "I don't understand. You seemed pretty against it... almost mad."

"Little rabbit, I could never be upset with you." Copeland kissed the tip of her nose. "But it was hot-as-Hades seeing you get all bossy."

"That was all an act?" Charlee pushed against his chest as she sat up and glowered down at him. "Just to mess with me?"

"No." Copeland rolled to his side and propped himself up with an elbow. "Because it pleased you to tell me what to do. And having the power of a horse-sized wolf ready to do your bidding thrilled you."

Her cheeks blossomed a brilliant crimson.

He was right. She'd liked having control. My heart ached as I realized it was something she'd never had back at her burrow.

Chapter TWELVE

CHARLEE

opeland sat up. Threading his fingers through my hair, he pulled my mouth close to his.

"Tell me I'm wrong and I'll apologize." His lips brushed against mine as he spoke.

I could try to deny it, but he was telling the truth. For the first time in my life, I'd felt brave, powerful, and in control. I'd felt safe and untouchable.

Either of the wolves could have snapped me like a twig or ripped out my vocal cords, yet they'd let me believe I was in charge. Even though I was trapped in a room with two larger-than-life wolves, I didn't experience a fraction of the fear that swamped my being every time I faced the council. It was a mind-bending fluster cluck.

"I liked it. A lot." My words were almost too soft to hear. "Control isn't something I'm used to possessing."

Copeland's deep laugh sent a wave of slick heat straight

between my thighs. "Obeying orders isn't something wolves are good at, unless those orders come from their alpha. But our wolves are eager to please you, and we'll happily follow your every command."

Linc's large wolf circled us, rubbing against my back as Copeland brushed his lips against mine in a featherlight kiss.

"And let me tell you a secret," Copeland murmured against my skin as his lips traveled down my neck. "I was jealous of how much attention Linc was getting, so I took a gamble on the fastest way to steal your focus and it paid off."

"Are you serious?" I spluttered, pushing away from him while trying to hide a laugh. "You're awful!"

"It worked." Copeland shrugged. "And I have no shame."

"How dare you interrupt my tummy rubs! I demand more." Linc's human arms wrapped around my waist and pulled me against his chest.

I jumped in surprise, shocked that I hadn't noticed him shift.

He spun me around so that I straddled his lap.

His very naked lap.

Linc's strong fingers circled my wrists, pulling them forward so that my hands rested against his chest. "But this time in my human form."

He began moving my hands so that they slid over his pecs and down his abs. My breath caught as I tried to wrap my head around the fact that this inhumanely beautiful man desired me. I'd thought my first experience with sex would be with balding, overweight men who were at least a couple of decades older than me. Instead, I was with a man who might as well have been a fallen angel.

"Your heat is building strength again." Linc laid back on the stack of blankets and grinned up at me. "We don't want to risk you being in pain any more than you need to. So take what you want. Use me."

It was too tempting an offer to pass up.

THE NEXT WEEK passed in a blur of sex, snacks, and sleep. If I ignored the constant underlying discomfort from the heat, it was the best honeymoon a girl could've asked for. Still, it was a relief when the demands of my heat eased.

Sneaking from the bed required me to maneuver over and under various limbs as though I were trying to sneak through security lasers in a museum. When my feet touched the wood floor, I headed into the bathroom to brush my teeth and run a comb through my hair.

Everything in the house had been designed for men who definitely had an advantage in the inches department—and I wasn't just talking about their thrill drills. I was forced to go up on tiptoe to see my reflection in the mirror.

Leaning close, I studied my eyes. The feverish glaze had disappeared, leaving them clear and bright. The dusting of freckles across my nose and cheeks stood out against my pale skin, and my cheekbones were slightly too sharp thanks to the weight I'd lost.

That worried me, and I quickly pulled the collar of my shirt from my neck. Glancing down, I peeked inside and groaned. I wasn't completely flat, but although I was still a rabbit, no one was going to be calling me Jessica. *Why is it that every time a woman loses weight, it's the boobs that vanish first?*

Letting go of the collar, I lifted the hem of the shirt. My hip bones stuck out and I could count my ribs thanks to the prominent indentations. I sighed, knowing it was going to take time for my body to recover, but hating it just the same.

Hearing the creak of the bathroom door, I turned and found Linc watching me from the doorway. His hair stuck out at odd angles, giving him a harmless innocence that couldn't be further from the truth. He gave me a sleepy smile that had my heart fluttering wildly. A sensation I didn't recognize flooded my chest, nearly choking me.

Happiness.

Running across the wooden floor, I threw myself at him.

He grunted, surprised by the attack. "Good morning to you, too." He swept me up into his arms.

I laughed, covering his face in kisses, drawing an amused rumble from his chest.

Linc tilted his head to the side like a confused puppy. "You don't smell like you're in heat. So what has a wild hair up your butt?"

Leaning back, I narrowed my eyes. "Are you making a hare joke?"

"I wasn't, but I will definitely use that in the future." Linc cupped my face and stroked his thumb along my cheekbone. "So are you planning to tell me what's going on?"

"Nothing." I relaxed into his palm, enjoying his touch. "It's just that I'm… I'm happy."

Linc studied me for a long time, neither of us breaking the silence.

Finally, I cleared my throat. "Do you think it's safe for us to go outside? I've been cooped up inside for far too long. I'm dying to get some fresh air, sunshine, and to explore my new home!"

His face lit with a genuine smile that reached all the way to his eyes. "Absolutely. Let's grab some breakfast and head out."

"You aren't leaving without us!" Copeland called from the bedroom. He threw back the covers on his side of my mattress nest and sat up. "I'll pack a picnic and we can eat by the lake."

"There's a lake nearby?" I asked.

Copeland nodded, stretching his arms above his head. "A small one. It's bigger than a pond, but smaller than what most people think of when they imagine a lake."

I squealed, unable to hide my excitement. "Swimming is one of my favorite things!"

"Rabbits can swim?" Linc asked.

"Of course we can!" I squirmed out of his arms and ran to kiss my other two mates.

"Huh." Copeland and Linc said in unison.

"Why is everyone so surprised by that? Rabbits are great swimmers," I huffed.

"And Charlee was the best swimmer in the burrow," Fletcher added, beaming with pride and pulling me into his lap. "Although, once she knows where the lake is, we may never see her again."

Scrambling off Fletcher's lap, I grabbed his and Copeland's hands and began dragging them from the bedroom. "Come on, Linc! Let's go!"

"Slow down, sugar." He followed us toward the kitchen. "It's not far. You'll have plenty of time to swim."

I knew he was right, but after days spent trapped in a cave and the bedroom, I was on the verge of going stir crazy. Thankfully, breakfast was quick, and we were out the door a half hour later.

I'D THOUGHT we'd be taking a nice stroll to the lake, but the men had unanimously decided that I didn't need to burn any more energy than was absolutely necessary. So instead, they were giving me a tour of the land around their home from my perch on Copeland's broad back. I'd heard of horseback tours, but never wolfback.

Sitting astride the brown and white wolf, my fingers desperately gripped his fur as he wove between trees and leaped over fallen logs. From the corner of my eye, I caught a blur of black and white as Fletcher darted through the thick undergrowth with the athletic ease only a rabbit could manage. Linc's chocolate brown wolf followed just behind us, a picnic basket clasped in his jaws.

The thick wall of trees parted, and we bounded into an open field. Tall grass sparkled with dew as it waved gently in the breeze. As we ran, the wolves stirred up a myriad of tiny insects and pollen around us. With the canopy of trees no longer covering the ground, the morning sun warmed my skin and caused Copeland's wolf to sneeze with enough violence to nearly toss me from his back.

"Ah!" I shrieked, stooping low to cling tighter to him.

Tumbling off his back while he was standing still wouldn't hurt, but at the speed he was running, it sure wasn't going to feel great to face plant in the dirt. Copeland barked in amusement and twisted his head to lick my face where I'd tucked it against his neck.

Linc's wolf picked up speed, running alongside us. His brown fur was dusted in enough pollen to make him look like an old man. He sneezed, sending more pollen dancing in the air, and I couldn't help but snicker when Copeland answered with a string of three sneezes in a row. Who knew wolves could have grass allergies?

Five minutes later, his footsteps slowed, and I pushed up into a sitting position to study the landscape. Jade-colored water stretched out in front of us, and although I could see the hazy shore on the far side of the lake, it was a lot further away than I'd anticipated. It wasn't much smaller than the lake I'd enjoyed swimming in whenever I snuck away from the burrow for some alone time.

"It's bigger than I expected!" I breathed.

"That's what she said."

I turned just in time to catch Linc's wink. He'd shifted and was pulling several pairs of shorts from the basket. He tossed a pair toward Fletcher, who strode out from the thick grass in his human form.

"That's odd." Fletcher rubbed his jaw, his expression serious. "That's not what I remember her saying the first time she saw you two naked."

I choked on a laugh. This earned me a grumpy huff from Copeland, and he abruptly planted his butt on the ground, sending me toppling from his back onto the ground, where I continued to giggle.

Tossing his shorts onto a nearby rock, Linc closed the distance between us. "You think that's funny, little rabbit?" His voice was rough and his eyes glinted with menace, but I could see the corner of his mouth twitching as he fought a smile.

Biting the inside of my cheek, I tried my best to appear serious. "Yeah, I kinda thought wolves would be bigger."

Fletcher howled with laughter, while Copeland hurried to shift, and Linc stormed toward me. Leaping to my feet, I took off, dumping my borrowed clothes to the pebble-covered shore as I ran for the water.

"But don't worry! It's not the size of the boat, but the

motion of the ocean that matters!" I tossed the words over my shoulder as I dove into the lake and swam as though my life depended on it... because maybe it did.

The shock of the cool mountain water had my chest tightening and sent chills racing over my skin. Popping to the surface, I gasped and sucked in a deep breath. Glancing toward the shore, I spotted my wolf shifters plunging into the water in pursuit.

Fletcher collapsed on the shore, holding his side as he continued to cackle. "Swim, Charlee! Swim! Don't let them get you!"

Giving him a saucy salute, I paused just long enough to pack my lungs with air before disappearing beneath the surface. I wasn't worried. Because unless the men were professional swimmers, they would struggle to catch me.

Opening my eyes, I kicked my legs and descended. The lake was pristine, reminding me of the beautiful water I'd seen in the travel magazines I'd occasionally found buried in the recycling bin outside one of the councilman's houses.

Rolling to my side, I looked back to see Copeland and Linc trying to follow me. They only made it about fifteen feet down before needing to resurface. Reaching the bottom of the lake about twenty-five feet down, I let myself relax. By concentrating on slowing my heartbeat, I could explore longer before needing to surface.

My mind quieted, and a sense of peace settled over me. It had been far too long since I'd been able to swim, plus my muscles were still shaky from everything over the past weeks, so I was forced to kick my way upward far sooner than I wished. I broke the surface about ten feet behind the pair of shouting wolf shifters.

"Don't ever do that again! You could have drowned!" Copeland bellowed.

"Are you sure you're a rabbit shifter and not a kraken?" Linc demanded, completely serious.

Treading water, I laughed and wiped the water from my eyes. "You saw my rabbit form, so you know what I am."

"Impossible! I nearly drowned three times while trying to reach you on the bottom!" Copeland protested, swimming toward me.

"I think we should do a closer inspection and find out where she's been hiding her gills," Linc suggested, paddling beside Copeland.

There was a glint in his eye that told me exactly what type of inspection he was planning to carry out, but I didn't plan to get caught. Not yet anyway...

"Fletcher!" I shouted at my mate, who lay sunbathing on the pebbled shore. "Did you know wolf shifters doggy paddle just like a puppy?" I was stirring the pot, but I was far too high on happiness to care.

He pushed up on his elbows and shook his head. "You are asking for trouble, Charlee."

Eyeing the wolves as they power-paddled toward me, I grinned. "You guys are so cute! Such good boys!" I cooed, waiting for them to get closer.

"We're going to do a different type of paddling when we catch you!" Linc promised with a teasing growl.

Right before the pair got close enough to grab me, I

ducked beneath the water and swam away. We spent the next thirty minutes playing a game of cat-and-mouse, or rather, bunny-and-beast.

Growing bored of simply staying out of reach, I changed tactics. I popped up in front of Copeland, who tried to cover his scream of surprise with a curse.

"Charlee! Are you trying to give me a heart attack?"

"Nope! I just wanted to talk to you about your car insurance—" I didn't get to finish my sentence before having to dart underwater to avoid him.

A handful of minutes later, I sneaked up behind Linc and pinched his adorable butt. He hadn't been expecting to be attacked from below, and although it was muffled, there was no missing his shout. I pressed my lips together, struggling to keep from expelling my air in a fit of giggles.

While I would've happily stayed in the lake for several hours, my muscles trembled from the exertion. Reluctantly, I headed toward shore. Within a minute, I could hear the splashing of the shifters as they raced after me. The water was still over my head when an arm curled around my waist, yanking me backward against a hard chest.

"And where do you think you are going, naughty bunny?" Copeland asked, his lips brushing my ear.

"To shore?" It came out as more of a question than a statement. "My legs are tired," I added, trying to elicit some pity and hopefully escape the consequences of my actions.

"We can't have that." Linc appeared in front of me. Since he was taller, the water circled around his abs. It dripped from his hair, running in rivulets down his shoulders and chest. "Let me help."

Gripping my thighs, he gently pried my legs apart and stepped between them. I found myself suspended in the water between the pair.

"Relax. We've got you. You don't need to do a thing," Copeland purred, his tongue swirling against my neck.

Linc's hands moved to cup my bare breasts. "I think we need to remind her how big wolves are."

As if I could forget when Copeland's hard length was literally grinding against my back, and the water was doing nothing to cool the heat of Linc's erection where it was branding my stomach.

"I think we should," Copeland agreed, his hands trailing over my skin, warming me despite the chill of the water.

Chapter
THIRTEEN

CHARLEE

"Here? Now?" I squeaked as Linc stroked a thumb along my slit.

"Yes, sugar." Linc lowered his head and nipped my lower lip. "I need you. Now." His length jerked against my belly.

"What if someone is hiking and sees us?" I protested, albeit weakly.

"No one comes to this lake," Copeland assured me, brushing my wet hair to the side so he could suck and nip the back of my neck. "Besides, anyone would be lucky to get to watch a woman as gorgeous as you getting her body worshiped."

"It is a beautiful thing to witness." Fletcher's voice came from the shore.

Peeking around the wall of muscle in front of me, I found my rabbit mate stroking the tent in his shorts. It was hot, and my insides quivered in excitement. Linc chose that moment to slip a finger inside me, making it impossible for me to speak.

Gasping, I leaned my head back against Copeland's chest and soaked in the delicious heat of my mates' bodies pressed against mine. Was their skin always this hot?

"Bunny boy, how about you come join us?" Copeland called.

Without question, Fletcher entered the lake and waded toward us.

"Kneel down," Linc ordered him.

The guys moved to where the water lapped against Fletcher's collarbones. I guess the wolves were communicating mentally because they moved as if they shared a single mind, all without speaking a word. Linc stepped to the side, letting Copeland fully support me as he shifted our positions so that Fletcher was in the water directly in front of me.

"Wrap your legs around his shoulders," Copeland whispered, his tongue tracing the curve of my ear.

My eyes widened. Oral wasn't something Fletcher and I had done yet. What if he wasn't into it? "You don't have to—"

"I want to," Fletcher cut me off, reaching out and sliding my legs around his neck.

His hands cupped my butt as he guided me to his mouth. Running his tongue along my aching slit, Fletcher made a sound that was a cross between a purr and the sound I make when eating a particularly decadent dessert.

Fletcher didn't need any further guidance from the wolves. Pulling me tighter against his mouth, his tongue slipped inside me, stroking and exploring. My insides quivered and sent a flush of desire straight between my legs. Instead of backing off, Fletcher hummed in delight and lapped up every drop as though it was a prize he'd earned.

Unable to help it, I squirmed, leaning back as I tried to escape the intensity of the sensations he was sparking through me.

"Oh no you don't," Copeland scolded.

Rather than letting me escape, he stepped forward, pressing me harder against Fletcher's eager mouth. With Copeland helping to keep me in place, Fletcher let one hand slip from where it had grasped my butt.

"But I can't breathe," I gasped.

Copeland's deep laugh would have made a villain proud. "Then it's a good thing we both know how long you can hold your breath."

Linc reappeared at my side. "Have we told you lately how sexy you are?" Bending down, he swirled his tongue around the hardened peak of my nipple.

"Mmhmm," Copeland agreed, his hand trailing down my ribs. "Every little thing about you is perfect."

Just that morning, I'd stared in the mirror and hadn't liked what I'd seen. But it was hard not to feel like a goddess when I could see the lust and love in my mates' eyes and feel it in their every touch. While I saw all the things I wished I could change, Copeland claimed they saw perfection.

Fletcher had been paying attention to my every reaction as he tasted me for the first time, and he proved to be a fast learner. Within minutes, I was panting and being driven toward bliss. Linc's tongue lavished attention on my nipple and breast, while Fletcher pressed two of his fingertips against my clit. In perfect harmony, as though they were conducting an orchestra where I was the only instrument, my mates continued to pleasure me until I had the most mind-shattering orgasm of my life.

"Charlee," Fletcher groaned my name.

Glancing down through the haze of lust, I noticed his heavy-lidded eyes and the flash of movement in the water. It took a moment for me to comprehend the reason his hand had disappeared from my butt. While he'd been devouring me, he'd been stroking himself and had joined me with his own release. I was still riding the high of my climax, but that didn't stop my body from clenching with renewed desire.

"Take us to the shallows." I was the one giving the orders now.

The moment we made it to where the water met the shore and was only a few inches deep, I looked at Linc. "Sit down."

Linc followed my direction, and Copeland lowered me to my feet. Kneeling in front of Linc, I gently pushed his chest, so he fell back. I wiggled between his legs, loving the way his eyes sparkled as he tried to figure out what new game we were playing. His laughter turned to a moan when I wrapped my lips around the head of his erection and took him deep into my mouth.

His hand moved to my head. He didn't apply pressure, but simply cradled it almost tenderly.

"Charlee." Linc's husky rasp sent chills over my skin and wet heat rushing between my thighs.

Lust surged through me, demanding to be filled. Keeping my forearms on the ground between Linc's legs, I went up on my knees and wiggled my behind in invitation to the man standing over me. I wasn't sure how skilled Copeland was at lipreading, but the man was a fantastic butt reader.

Copeland lined himself up with my entrance, and gripping my hips to support me, he pushed inside me. There was no resistance thanks to how soaked I was, and I moaned in ecstasy as his cock sank deep—or at least, I tried to moan. It was hard to vocalize when your mouth was full.

My tongue swirled along Linc's length, while Copeland rolled his hips in an erotic rhythm. With each thrust, my belly tightened as the need for release built. Linc's breathing grew more ragged, my muffled sounds of pleasure seemed to be driving him crazy.

"Copeland," Linc growled, tone harsh.

I didn't know if it was a warning that he wasn't going to last, or an order for Copeland to put me out of my misery. Either way, without breaking his pace, Copeland reached around my hip and pressed his fingers against me.

That added bit of friction was too much, and two hard thrusts later, I fell apart. Taking Linc deep into my mouth, I swallowed hard. I wanted him to feel the muscles of my throat clenching around him as my body clenched around Copeland.

My men came hard, their cocks jerking as they joined me in pure pleasure. When the last of the aftershocks faded, Linc pulled me onto his chest, while Fletcher and Copeland collapsed on the ground beside us. We lay there, letting the sun warm our skin and listening to the water lazily lapping at the shore.

"Can we do this every day?" I mumbled against Linc's chest, struggling to stay awake.

"Absolutely," Linc mumbled sleepily.

Copeland released a string of sneezes then laughed. "I'm down, but next time maybe we'll take the forest path instead of the field."

"Do wolves have allergies?" I asked, lazily circling my fingertips over Linc's skin. "And are you guys always this scorching hot?" Their skin hadn't seemed abnormally hot when we'd first met, but then again, I'd been in heat so I might not have noticed.

"If you'd asked me yesterday, I would've said no," Copeland paused, this time to cough, "but now I'm not so sure. To answer your second question; yes, we're always hot." He wiggled his eyebrows suggestively.

Fletcher snorted and tossed a shirt in Copeland's face. The wolf winked at me, then rolled the cloth up to use as a pillow and closed his eyes.

Less than five minutes later, both wolves had fallen asleep.

Fletcher caught my hand and brought the back of it to his lips. "Where is all that amazing wolf stamina they were bragging about? A swim, sex, and sunshine was all it took to knock them out cold. I can't wait to rub this in."

We lapsed into a peaceful silence, enjoying the freedom of being outdoors and not needing to look over our shoulders. I could definitely get used to this.

Chapter FOURTEEN

CHARLEE

I t was mid-afternoon by the time we'd made it home from the lake. My wolves had grown progressively tired as we'd eaten our picnic, and I'd refused to let them carry me back to the house. Instead, we'd taken our time and walked back on foot. With each step, Linc and Copeland moved slower and their skin shone with a sweaty sheen.

Both men had assured me they were just tired from not sleeping well the past few days, and all they needed was a nap and they'd be fine. But holding the cool, wet cloth to their foreheads, and watching their breathing grow more ragged with each passing minute, I couldn't deny the truth any longer. My wolves were sick.

I snuck from the bedroom and found Fletcher sitting at the dining room table. He stood, motioning for me to take a seat.

"How are they?" he asked, grabbing a plate from the refrigerator with a sandwich that he sat in front of me. "I know you're stressed, but you need to eat."

"Their temperatures are dangerously high. They don't want to go to the doctor or worry the alpha, but we can't wait around doing nothing while they get worse." My eyes burned with unshed tears as I picked at the food. "I still don't understand how it's possible for a shifter to get sick. Our immune systems work too fast."

Fletcher, who'd been pale and withdrawn the last hour, sat down across from me. "Because they don't have a virus or bacteria."

"You've seen them! What else could it be?" I pressed my fingertips against my eyes, rubbing furiously.

"Toxin."

That single word hit me like a physical blow.

"A… t-toxin?" I croaked. "If that were true, we'd be sick too!"

"Because that's how Blackberry Burrow protects its borders from predators." Fletcher propped his elbows on the table and dropped his face into his hands. "It's why we aren't really bothered. I'm a little tired, but nothing like what the wolves are dealing with. They learned some rabbits are resistant, or able to tolerate a significant amount of certain toxic compounds like pyrrolizidine alkaloids and atropine. Those can be found in some plants that are lethal in mammals, like cats and dogs…"

"And wolf shifters," I breathed in horror.

"Yes. They've found a way to enhance those compounds

in the medical facility, making them far more dangerous for predators, as well as figuring out how to increase the odds that rabbit shifters can survive constant exposure." Fletcher refused to meet my eyes as he spoke.

"Why did you only think to mention any of this now?" I hissed. "If we'd known, maybe we could have prevented this! Were you trying to protect those monsters? Even after everything they did to me?"

My chest heaved, and for the first time in my life, I found myself truly angry with Fletcher. We'd had disagreements and spats over the years, but I wasn't sure I'd ever be able to forgive him if my wolf mates died.

"You know I'd never protect the burrow! My only loyalty is to you." Fletcher's hands fell from his face and he peered up at me with a look of devastation in his red eyes. "The burrow uses their toxin as a barrier to keep rogue wolves and coyotes from attacking us. Almost like a salt circle to keep a ghost away. I didn't realize they would weaponize it outside of their border."

I stared at Fletcher, utterly speechless. "Why didn't I know about this? I grew up in Blackberry Burrows. I think I'd have known if there was a toxic barrier." Standing, I began to pace.

Fletcher shook his head. "They didn't want anyone to find out. I don't even know the details, and I'm the son of one of their leaders. The council fears what would happen to them if the wolf packs discover they've created a toxin that could be used against them."

My knees buckled, and I sagged back down into a chair. "How did they do it?"

Fletcher gave a long sigh. "I don't know the full details. I ran across some documents right before we left. I was looking for some kind of leverage in the hopes they'd be willing to barter my silence for your freedom."

My heart gave a little tug at those words and some of my anger cooled. He had risked so much for me, while having no promise of having his sacrifice or devotion returned.

"A lot of the information on the documents was redacted. But from what I gathered, they created a formula using their toxin that they used to drench the ground around the burrows, allowing the plants to soak it up."

"So, it's like a systemic pesticide, but instead of for pests, it's for our predators?" I asked, my voice rising in incredulity. How far was the council willing to go to keep their secrets? "But that would only work if they ate it, and I doubt most wolves are out munching on random shrubbery."

Fletcher shook his head. "No, they don't have to eat it. They just have to break the branches as they run through in their wolf forms. It can be ingested, as well as absorbed through the skin. If it gets into their mouths, skin, eyes, or covers their fur, which they later lick, it kills them. It's sophisticated and cunning and exactly what I would expect from our council. They've even manipulated the plants to do their dirty work."

I wanted my freedom, but not if it required me to exchange my mates' lives in order to gain it.

"That explains how they could poison any wolves that attacked the burrow, but it doesn't explain how they got to Copeland and Linc." Grinding my teeth, I fought the urge to scream in frustration.

"I don't know the answer to that either." Fletcher cursed and banged his fist on the arm of the chair. "From the document I read, it takes multiple treatments over many weeks to reach toxic levels in the test plants. There's no way they could've snuck onto the lands enough times to raise those levels. Besides, we haven't even been here that long."

He was right, which meant they had found another way to use the toxin. We hadn't even gone out where there were groups of people where someone could've bumped into them like a secret agent from a spy movie and injected them.

"Could they have tampered with the water supply?" I asked.

Fletcher stared at the floor, mulling over the suggestion. "No. The amount they would've needed to poison that much water would be impossible to sneak into pack lands without being caught."

We fell into silence, both of us racking our brains and trying to figure out how the wolves could have been exposed. I thought back over the last few hours; the guys making me breakfast, swimming and making love in the lake, our slow walk back home where we crashed into bed.

Nothing stood out.

Not until I remembered the field.

It had been so beautiful. The wolves running through the towering flowers and grass while brilliant butterflies and tiny finches took flight. The petals had fallen around us, as pollen had clung to the wolves' fur.

"It wasn't pollen," I whispered, my voice trembling.

"What?" Fletcher asked.

But even as he asked, I could see the realization dawning on him as well. They'd turned their toxin into a powder. How had they known we would go through the wildflower field?

They couldn't have known.

Which means they had probably spread it all around the cabin.There was no way of knowing how many acres of the woods and fields surrounding us had been dusted in the stuff.

"We can't let any of the pack members come up here and risk being exposed to the toxin. How are we going to get the men to the hospital?" The few bites of sandwich I'd swallowed were doing their best to come back up.

"I found the keys to their Jeep. If necessary, we'll force the wolves to let us take them to the hospital." Seeing my distress, Fletcher moved around the table to wrap his arms around my shoulders.

"I don't think it will take much force. They are barely responding right now," I croaked, my voice breaking.

Fletcher kissed the top of my head. "Don't stress too much, Charlee. Wolves are one of the most powerful shifters in the paranormal world. Their immune systems are probably just working to destroy the toxin. The pack doctors will give them fluids that will help flush the toxin out quicker."

"But what if the hospital can't? What if they fail? What if Copeland and Linc die?" Tears slid down my cheeks. "I've brought them nothing but trouble."

Fletcher squatted beside me. "Stop that. The guys would probably flip you over their knees and spank you if they heard you talking like that."

He picked up a chip from my plate and held it to my lips. "Open. You have to get some food in you before we leave."

"You aren't going to feed me like I'm a toddler—"

"Hush." Fletcher shoved the chip into my mouth. "I wanted you to myself, but I knew you'd need more than I'd be able to provide by myself to survive your heats. Watching those arrogant wolf-men make love to you the first time just about broke me."

Shocked at the admission, I obediently opened my mouth for another bite, not wanting to interrupt him.

"Everything inside me was screaming that they were nothing but horny dogs seizing the opportunity to get some action. I kept my mouth shut because I didn't have a choice if I wanted you to survive." He cut a bit off the sandwich, feeding it to me before continuing. "But when I pushed past those feelings of jealousy, I realized I'd been wrong. I recognized the look in their eyes because I've seen it in my face when I look in the mirror. It was the same with the way they touch you; I knew they were just as drawn to you, just as in love with you, as I am."

Swallowing the bite, I started to speak, but Fletcher shoved another bite into my mouth.

"I'm telling you this so that you will stop feeling guilty. You didn't set fire to the woods, you didn't hire coyotes to attack the cave, and you had nothing to do with the toxin. Copeland and Linc are big boys who can make their own decisions, and they've made it clear"—Fletcher tapped a finger against the wolves' marks on either side of my neck —"that you belong to them. To us. We are a family now, and we'll face whatever comes together."

"Thank you," I sobbed, throwing my arms around his neck, nearly toppling us onto the floor.

"You have nothing to thank me for." Fletcher patted my back, then grabbed a clean napkin from the table. "Now dry those tears and let's get your wolves to the Jeep."

Chapter FIFTEEN

CHARLEE

I had expected the men to put up a fight, but the fact that they didn't was a testament to how sick they truly were. By the time we got them into the Jeep, and were headed to the pack house, both Fletcher and I were soaked in sweat, and I was pretty sure I'd pulled at least three muscles.

Neither Copeland nor Linc could keep their eyes open, and the few words they mumbled were barely intelligible. I tried to get them to let the alpha know we were headed to the hospital, but they'd been too out of it to even understand what I was asking. Instead, we decided to go straight to the pack house and hope they'd know how to help or the fastest way to the nearest hospital.

"They need something to bring down their fevers," I told Fletcher, my eyes darting from the back seat out the front window. "Shifters can tolerate a lot more than a human, but having temperatures this high for prolonged periods isn't good. They're dehydrated from vomiting up everything I've tried to give them, and both their breathing and heart rates are fluctuating wildly. They're going downhill so fast." I looked out the window, trying to hide the fresh wave of tears.

"Worrying isn't going to help anything." Fletcher kept his voice calm, trying to be reassuring, but it didn't fool me.

His fingers were gripping the steering wheel with such force that his knuckles had turned white, and his jaw was clenched so tightly I was surprised he hadn't cracked any teeth. It definitely wasn't just me who was worried.

Fletcher focused on navigating the unfamiliar curvy mountain road while I listened to the men's increasingly labored breathing. The minutes ticked by as we remained silent, lost in our thoughts, but as we neared the main center of the pack, rows of houses came into view. We passed an elementary school, a row of businesses with people bustling in and out, before—at last—the pack house loomed in front of us.

"Wait here." Fletcher was out of the Jeep and banging on the pack house door before I'd even unbuckled my seat belt.

A tall man with dark brown-hair answered the door, listening as Fletcher explained what was going on. I twisted around in my seat, anxiously studying Copeland and Linc in the backseat. Their skin, which was normally a gorgeous sun-kissed tan, was a pale blue-gray. They clearly weren't getting enough oxygen, but I worried whether there could also be internal bleeding. Sweat dripped from their hair as though they'd been swimming, and their bodies trembled as the fever wreaked havoc.

I jumped when Fletcher yanked open my door. "Come on! They have a fully equipped infirmary inside the pack house."

"Will that be enough? They need a hospital." I scrambled from the car, warily eyeing the men and women pouring from the pack house to surround the vehicle.

"They've assured me it has every life-saving piece of equipment they might need. And if not, they will have a helicopter on standby to airlift them to the nearest hospital."

Still, I hesitated, blocking the handle to the back door, feeling protective of the wolves who'd already risked their lives for me.

"We have to trust them, Charlee," Fletcher insisted, gently moving me to the side so he could open the backseat. "They know wolf shifter anatomy far better than we do. This is the best chance Copeland and Linc have to pull through."

He was right, but it didn't make it any easier to watch unfamiliar wolf shifters remove my mates from the backseat and rush them inside—away from me.

I stood staring at the open pack house door, wanting to follow but unable to move. Being surrounded by complete strangers and the scent of so many wolf shifters was a lot to process. Despite my desire to be strong for my mates, my body began to tremble. These wolves had protected me from the coyotes, but my rabbit nature was screaming that I needed to bolt for safety.

A hand rested on my shoulder. "I know it's overwhelming, and the alarms blaring in your mind are claiming you're in danger. But it's not true. You're safe, Charlee."

I turned to find two women standing on either side of me, putting themselves between me and the gathered wolf shifters. The hand on my shoulder belonged to a woman with long dark hair, while the other had brilliant blue hair. They were the same height as me, making them far more petite than everyone else around us.

"Hi. I'm Monroe. We've been looking forward to meeting you, just not under these circumstances." The dark-haired woman gave me a sympathetic smile. "Come inside with us. We can sit in the waiting room until the doctors get Linc and Copeland settled into a room."

"You're both rabbit shifters," I murmured, allowing Monroe to lead me up the porch steps.

"Yep! And I'm Ellora." The blue-haired woman fell into step beside us.

"Charlee, you have no idea how excited we are to have another rabbit around. Our fluffles are amazing, but we can't help but miss being around our species as well." Monroe's smile reached all the way to her eyes, letting me know she was sincere.

"And it's not just us! Monroe's bestie, Reese, has been planning a BBQ bonfire to welcome you to the pack. Everyone has been looking forward to meeting the bunny who stole the hearts of the most stubborn mountain men the pack has ever seen. They might as well be hermits!" Ellora threw up her hands.

They were trying to distract me, and it had worked. At least for a moment. "So they aren't very social?"

Monroe snorted. "Let me put it this way. There are more sightings of Sasquatch than of either Linc or Copeland. My mate says they've always preferred the quiet of nature, but they did their best to adjust to crowds while trying to find a mate. That didn't work out, and they returned to the mountains. Your mates are good men."

"I know," I whispered.

And they're dying because of me, I thought, afraid to say it out loud.

They continued their friendly small talk as they led me inside, but I barely heard another word. All my attention was focused on the hall in front of us, searching for any sign of my wolves.

We turned into one of the open doorways, and it surprised me to find the room looked far more like a cozy reading nook than a hospital waiting area. Monroe settled me into a cushy recliner, while Ellora mentioned something about getting drinks before heading for the doorway, where she nearly ran into Fletcher and the tall man beside him. Power seemed to radiate from the stranger. I didn't need an introduction to know this was the alpha who'd fallen head-over-heels for a rabbit shifter.

"I'm going to Alpha Cillian's office while we wait for news on Linc and Copeland. Is that okay, or do you want me to stay with you?" Fletcher's brows drew together, his eyes swirling with turmoil and indecision.

He didn't want to leave my side any more than I wanted him to. But we both knew the alpha needed to be filled in on everything that was happening.

"Go ahead." I turned to Monroe. "You should go with them. It's information you need to be aware of, too." Seeing her hesitation, I nodded my chin toward the door. "Please, this is important for the safety of the pack."

Monroe stood, still reluctant to leave me. "Ellora will be right back…"

"It's okay. I'll be fine," I reassured her.

With that, they headed down the hall, leaving me alone with my chaotic thoughts and gut-wrenching fears. Kicking off the huge flip-flops I'd borrowed from Copeland, I tucked my legs against my chest and wrapped my arms around them. My eyes landed on the large grandfather clock in the corner and followed the second hand as it moved around the gold-plated face. It had been almost ten minutes when Ellora reappeared.

"Here we go." She was carrying a small tray and handed me a steaming mug of hot chocolate.

I took the offered drink, more to have something to do with my hands than from an eagerness to drink it. Any other time, I'd have loved the treat, but with my stomach churning as though it was making butter back in the 1800s, I wasn't sure I could keep anything down.

We sat in silence, listening to the clock tick away the passing minutes, before she spoke again. "If you're okay by yourself for a little while, I have a quick errand to run." Ellora chewed her bottom lip between her perfect white teeth, obviously torn about leaving me.

"I'm fine." Forcing a smile to my lips, I set my mug on the table next to me. "I think I'll try to take a quick nap while I wait for the doctors to give me an update. Last night was rough."

Ellora hopped from her seat and pulled me into a tight hug. "I can't even imagine what you're going through. Yes, try to sleep for a bit."

I thought I'd cried out all my tears, but my eyes instantly began to water. It was one thing to be treated with kindness from the men who were bound to me as mates, but it was something completely different to experience it from female shifters. I'd had plenty of female friends as a child, but as I started questioning things and then moved on to rebelling against the arbitrary rules, things had changed.

Worried that I'd be a bad influence, the older females did their best to limit the amount of time that was spent between my friends and myself. I knew I'd be punished for challenging the council's authority, but despite that, I found it impossible to keep my head down and my mouth closed. Anyone perceived to be my ally or friend would face similar consequences, so I didn't blame the other girls for avoiding me as we grew older.

Ellora grabbed a throw blanket from a basket on the floor and tucked it around me. My chest warmed as I watched her bright blue ponytail swing with each step she took as she left the room. It had been less than an hour, but I already knew Monroe and Ellora were going to be amazing friends. My life had changed so much in such a short time.

I could be happy here… as long as I have my mates at my side.

Overwhelmed by mental and physical exhaustion, I closed my eyes and dropped my head back against the leather chair.

Chapter
SIXTEEN

CHARLEE

I must have dozed off, because the next thing I heard was the sound of soft whispers. I slowly opened my eyes, then bolted upright in confusion, not remembering where I was.

"Hey, it's okay." Monroe leaned forward, catching my frantic gaze. "You were asleep. We're still in the waiting area."

My galloping heart slowed as the room and the two women sitting in the chairs on either side of me came into focus. "Linc? Copeland? How are they?"

The corner of Monroe's mouth turned down in a frown. "Nothing the doctors have tried has made any difference. Fletcher told us everything he knows, and we informed the medical staff, but they simply don't know where to even start." Seeing my distress, she was quick to add, "Don't lose hope! They are still alive, and that's the most important thing. No one is going to give up trying to save them."

I swallowed hard, unable to speak. I'd feel a lot better if we knew more about what we were dealing with, but it wasn't like Blackberry Burrow was going to hand over records to the pack about a weapon they'd created specifically to kill wolves.

Ellora cleared her throat and bent to snatch a bag from the floor. "I'm sure you'll want to visit the shops and pick out stuff, but I couldn't resist grabbing a couple of outfits so you could at least be more comfortable. Since no one has seen you shopping in town yet, we figured the men were probably keeping you hostage." Her eyes twinkled with a knowing look. "If I weren't so stubborn, I think mine would still be holding me hostage."

Monroe nodded. "Yes. I thought being married to the alpha was tough, but Ellora's mate, Mac, takes the prize for pure bossiness."

They were back to trying to distract me. Needing to think about anything other than losing my mates, I appreciated it. "Mac?"

"Yes. He can be a little intimidating." Ellora rolled her eyes. "But he's an absolute teddy bear when you get to know him."

"I'm sure you're right, but everyone is too terrified to get close enough to find out," Monroe teased.

Ellora laughed. "That's probably true!"

"Maybe when the guys are feeling better, we can have a

girls' day out," Monroe suggested. "That could be a lot of fun."

Since I had never been on a girls' day out, I had no idea if it would be fun or not. But I thought I would enjoy spending the day with them when I wasn't so stressed about my mates.

"Here." Ellora handed me a glossy pink shopping bag. "There's a bathroom across the hallway. You can go in there and change. We're about the same size, so I think everything should fit."

"Are you sure?" I reached out to take the bag but stopped, hesitating.

It would be nice to wear clothes that actually fit, but I didn't have money to reimburse her.

"You might as well take them because she won't take no for an answer." Monroe twisted the cap off a water bottle and took a sip.

"She's right," Ellora agreed, completely unapologetic. "I'm stubborn."

"It seems like that might be a rabbit shifter trait," I half-heartedly joked, taking the bag.

"Hmm." Monroe rubbed her chin and pretended to be deep in thought. "You might be on to something."

Following Ellora's directions, I found the bathroom. I quickly slipped out of the oversized shirt and untied the short's drawstring I'd been forced to pull tight and wrap around my waist twice just to keep them up.

The blue jeans she'd bought were brand new, but were buttery soft and faded, as though they'd been well worn.

They fit perfectly, far better than any pair of hand-me-down pants I'd owned in the burrow. Reaching into the bag, I found a petal pink shirt that was made from the softest fibers I'd ever touched. Curious, I checked the label.

"Bamboo? You can wear bamboo?" I asked the empty bathroom. "Who knew?"

In the bottom of the bag, I found a sports bra, pink socks with a pattern of tiny white bunnies, and a pair of white slip-on sneakers. Within five minutes, I was fully dressed. Ellora had thoughtfully picked everything to be comfortable, the type of clothing you could forget you were wearing.

I moved to the sink to splash water on my face. When I finished, I felt somewhat human again.

Ellora clapped her hands together as I stepped back into the waiting room. "Oh! They fit perfectly!"

"I don't think I've worn anything this comfortable before." Feeling shy, I bent and gave her a tentative hug. "Thank you."

"Don't even mention it!" She wrapped her arms around me, giving me a tight squeeze.

Before we could say anything more, there was a soft tap on the door and the sound of footsteps behind us. I turned just in time to bump into Fletcher's chest.

"Hi, love." Fletcher pulled me into a tight hug.

I wasn't sure who needed the reassurance of being held by their mate more, Fletcher or me. Unwilling to let me go, Fletcher sat down and pulled me onto his lap.

Cillian stepped into the room and moved to place a soft kiss on the top of Monroe's head.

Monroe asked the question I was too afraid to voice. "Any changes?"

"No." Cillian shook his head. "Our doctors aren't equipped to handle something like this. But there's a hospital in Bradford, and a specialty team runs a private lab and facility inside it. They have extensive experience with wolf shifters, so we're hopeful they'll be able to figure out how to handle this."

The alpha turned toward me. "Charlee, a helicopter will land in the next few minutes to transport Linc and Copeland to the hospital. There's enough space in the helicopter for you to fly with them."

He was doing his best to comfort me, but he'd misread the pain on my face, thinking I was upset about being separated from them; it was something else entirely that had caused my heart to sink to my stomach.

"Thank you," I whispered.

Cillian nodded. "Fletcher, you can go with her. I'll follow later, but first, I need to travel to meet with the alphas of several packs in a nearby city. They need to be aware of the danger this toxin poses to their wolves, and they need to be there when I call the burrow and demand answers."

Fletcher looked at me and back at the alpha, clearly torn. "I want to go with Charlee, but—"

"It's fine," I cut Fletcher off, knowing he felt responsible, as though he should've foreseen how Blackberry Burrow would use the toxin. "It's not your fault. You should go with Cillian in case they have questions you can answer."

Fletcher rested his cheek on top of my head. "I know very little about it, but I'd like to help if I can."

This gave me the perfect out I was seeking, and I pounced on it. "Don't worry about me. I'm so tired that once they take the guys into the facility and start working on them, I'll probably just sleep."

Fletcher studied my face. "You promise to eat something? You're nowhere near recovered from everything—"

"I know, I know! And I will," I promised.

"Once they drop off Linc and Copeland, the helicopter will return to get Monroe and a couple of pack members. You won't be alone for more than a few hours, and there are several shifters among the staff who will help you should you need anything." Cillian glanced down at his phone. "The helicopter just landed. Let's go."

We followed the alpha down the corridor, where we met up with the staff rushing Linc and Copeland to the helipad. Out on the roof, we watched as they loaded the stretchers onto the helicopter.

Fletcher gave me a quick kiss. "I'll be back at your side before you realize it. Be safe."

"I will." It was a promise I hoped I could keep.

A guy in a flight uniform motioned for me to step closer and helped me up into the chopper. The well-trained team took mere minutes to strap down the metal stretcher frames and make sure they were secure. They checked my harness, then gave the pilot the okay to take off.

My stomach dipped and my stress levels rose as we lifted into the air. In my worry over my mates, I'd forgotten that I'd never flown before… and it wasn't something I'd had on my bucket list.

Free diving far beneath the water? Yes please.

Flying far above the land? No thanks.

I stared through the dust-covered window at the horizon. The sky had turned the rose-gold hue that signaled the sun was soon to set. Fresh grief pierced my heart, and I wished I were sitting by the lake, snuggling with my mates as we watched the beautiful sunset together.

Pushing aside my sadness, I forced myself to focus. I began a mental walk-through of my plan, wanting to be prepared the moment we touched down.

Bradford. I'd never been there, but I was familiar with its location on a map. Fletcher must have truly trusted the pack to protect me if he was allowing me to be taken to a city located not too far from our old burrow. Or had he been so distracted he hadn't heard where the hospital was located?

When Fletcher and I had left Blackberry Burrow, we'd made the journey on foot because we hadn't wanted to risk leaving a paper trail for the burrow to follow. That had meant no taxis, no airplanes, and no rideshares. We'd also spent most of that time in our rabbit forms to avoid the need for restaurants and hotels. Several times throughout that trip, Fletcher had hidden me away so he could spend several hours backtracking and creating false tracks in case anyone was after us.

In the end, it had taken about two weeks to get to Monroe's pack. Now, the helicopter was covering those miles in a matter of hours.

As the sun slowly sank toward the horizon, I rested my head against the window and watched the rise and fall of my mates' chests. Needing to touch them, but unable to move much thanks to my harness, I could only reach Copeland's hand. I laced my fingers with his, relieved to find his skin was much cooler than it had been at the house.

That relief was short-lived. What if that wasn't a good thing? For all I knew, it was a bad sign, especially since both men were nearly unresponsive.

Linc and Copeland hadn't roused as they were loaded into the helicopter, nor had they moved during the hours we'd been in the air. Had they given them a sedative? Or had the toxin caused them to be as motionless as statues?

I was too afraid to ask, and I wasn't sure I could handle the answer...not when I needed to be strong for what was coming.

Cillian planned to confront the burrow and demand answers from the council. But if that didn't work, they'd have to find a way to storm the gates and get the answers they needed from the scientists who'd created this toxin. But that would take time... something I wasn't sure my mates had.

Besides, how could they get onto burrow lands when there was a toxin that could poison them if they so much as brushed against the limbs of the plants that created the perimeter? What if the burrow had a way of blasting it onto the streets as well? None of us knew how much of the toxin they had stockpiled. Even if the wolf shifters stayed in their human forms and wore hazmat suits, the rabbits could have rogue coyotes waiting to attack and rip open the suits before they got across the perimeter.

The alpha would do whatever it took to save Copeland and Linc, but he couldn't risk the lives of the rest of his pack in the process. That meant he'd have to come up with a strategic plan rather than going in with metaphorical guns blazing.

For the first time in my life, I found myself in a strange position.

I had the advantage.

As a rabbit, I was apparently resistant to the burrow's toxin. I was also small, fast, and I knew just about every way to sneak in and out of burrow property.

I also had the element of surprise on my side. The council would be distracted from dealing with the angry werewolf alphas who were ready to declare war.

The very last thing they'd expect was for me to return alone. And yes, I was fully aware I was falling into the "stupid female tries to save the day" trope, but I didn't see any other option.

Fletcher would never have let me return to Blackberry Burrow. Not even if I had an army at my back. But if he tried to enter the front gate, I knew he'd be arrested on the spot. The council considered him a traitor, and they'd make him disappear before anyone could come looking for him.

That was why I had to be the one to go. It was far easier

for me to sneak in and out. Who would be watching for the one rabbit no one was expecting to return alone?

I already had a pretty good idea of which man was most likely to have the answers I needed. We'd met on more than one unpleasant occasion. His past repulsive behavior would make it easy to do whatever I had to, to get the answers I needed. I certainly wouldn't lose any sleep if he gained a few scars, considering how many he'd helped to carve into my skin.

Knowing there would be little opportunity to rest until I completed my mission, I closed my eyes and tried to sleep. But it was impossible while listening to the labored breathing of two of the three men I loved more than life itself.

As the lights of the city began twinkling in the distance, I squeezed Copeland's hand and committed every line of both men's faces to memory.

When we left the burrow, I promised myself I'd die before ever stepping foot there again. But now, I'd die before letting anything stop me from returning… or from making my way back to my mates. They'd fought a pack of rogue coyotes to save me, and I was more than willing to bop a few bunnies on the head if it meant saving them.

Chapter SEVENTEEN

CHARLEE

The moment the helicopter rails touched down on the roof of the hospital, doctors and nurses rushed from inside the building, ready to help move their patients inside. With the type of expertise that came from years of practice, the medical team on the helicopter swiftly unfastened the stretchers. They removed my mates, their I.V. equipment, and oxygen machines from the helicopter without tangling or tripping over a single cord or line.

I'd been worried the alpha might have assigned someone specifically to guard me, and I'd been trying to come up with excuses that would give me a chance to sneak away. Maybe I'd pretend to go to the bathroom, or make a private call. But I needn't have stressed over it.

As the staff worked like a well-oiled machine, moving

the men from the helicopter across the roof of the hospital, and through the hall to the private wing for shifters, I was swept along with them. They relayed information about my mates, no one paying me any attention. It was in that bustle that I found it easy to slip away.

Ducking into a doorway in the wide, stark white hallway, I held my breath as the staff rushed past. My lip wobbled as I took a last look at my mates' deathly pale faces. I prayed the doctors would figure out how to counteract the toxin, but I would not sit around and wait. Spinning on my heel, and without a backward glance, I headed for the stairwell and made my way down to the ground floor of the hospital.

The stairwell door opened into a parking garage, and I shivered. Was it just me, or did walking around a dark parking garage make everyone feel as though they were the lead actress in a horror film?

And why was there always a flickering overhead light adding to the terrifying ambience? Was that part of the garage building code, along with the depressing gray cement? Had anyone thought to suggest bright paint, disco ball lighting, and cheerful music?

Wrapping my arms around my waist, I wished I'd brought one of the guys' hoodies with me. I eyed every car with suspicion, feeling sure there could be a knife-wielding serial killer waiting to pop out. It reminded me of how much anxiety I'd had as a kid whenever I saw a Jack-in-the-box. A door slammed a few rows over, causing me to nearly leap out of my skin.

Deciding I didn't want to stick around to find out if I was going to get a podcast dedicated to me, I bolted. The moment I was on the street, I moved into the shadows, hoping to avoid security cameras as I headed down the sidewalk.

Once I was far enough from the hospital that I was pretty sure I wouldn't be immediately spotted by anyone who might have been sent to look for me, I slowed. Glancing up and down the street, I searched for a taxi or rideshare driver dropping off a passenger.

Bradford was a big city, and it would take a long time to get to the farthest side, which was in the direction of the burrow. The burrow was close enough that I could've made the walk on foot, but far enough that it would have taken most of the night to get there. By then, my absence would have been noticed… and it might have been too late for my mates.

A driver pulled up to a small Chinese restaurant a few feet from where I was standing. Two young women stepped out, laughing and chattering. The sticker on the back windshield marked the vehicle as being used as part of a rideshare company. *Bingo.*

I didn't have a phone I could use to book a ride, but I had some cash Fletcher had tucked in my pocket, and I hoped that would be enough to convince the driver to accept an off-the-books trip. Hurrying over before the car could pull away, I tapped my knuckles on the driver's side window.

Pushing away all my stress and worries, I forced an

easy-going smile to my lips. "I'm *sooo* sorry to bother you! My phone was stolen and now I can't call any of my friends to come pick me up. I can't even use the app to book a ride." I held up some of the cash. "Is there any way I could hire you to take me home? I have the money, and I can pay upfront for it."

The driver hesitated for only a moment before nodding. "Sure, I was about to get off anyway, so I don't see the harm in giving you a lift."

Clicking a button, I heard the locks click. "Hop in." She grinned up at me, jerking her thumb toward the backseat.

I scrambled inside, not wanting to give her a chance to change her mind.

The driver adjusted the rearview mirror so that our eyes met. "Alright. So where are we headed?"

I didn't exactly have an answer to that since females weren't allowed outside of the burrow, so I'd never visited Bradford. But I knew which direction I needed to head in.

Thinking on my feet, I pressed my fingers against my forehead, pretending to concentrate. "I just got into town yesterday, and I'm terrible with names. It's a big hotel on the north side of the city. Ugh! What is the name?"

The driver took pity on me. "Oh, you mean the new one they built just outside the city limit near the airport? Ford-moore Hotel is huge!"

And that was what I was going to go with…

"Yes, that's it! The Fordmoore!" I exclaimed, trying to sound relieved. "I'm so embarrassed."

"Oh, don't be." She laughed good-naturedly, putting the vehicle in drive and checking her mirrors before pulling out onto the street. "The absolute worst part about moving to a new city is trying to remember all the new streets and buildings! It's really easy to get turned around. Don't worry, though. You'll have it down pat in no time."

"I sure hope so." I sighed, leaning back in my seat as we merged with traffic and sped away.

She continued to babble cheerfully as I stared out the window, trying to memorize the unfamiliar street signs as they passed in a blur. I'd hoped I could use them to make my way back to the hospital, but after ten minutes, my head throbbed with the beginning of a migraine. Giving up, I decided I'd have to rely on finding another driver to take me to the hospital when I returned from my mission.

My palms grew sweaty as I played and replayed my plan in my mind. The pain of my heat had receded, but a new discomfort was pushing to the forefront thanks to the miles that stretched further and further between my mates and myself. The helicopter ride that carried me away from Fletcher had only been tolerable because of Copeland and Linc's presence.

Just focus on the mission, Charlee. The sooner I get answers, the sooner I'll be back with my mates.

"We're here," the driver chirped as she pulled into a parking place in front of a towering hotel.

Scooting to the right passenger door, I pulled the handle and stepped onto the sidewalk. Turning, I reached through the open passenger side window and held out a wad of cash toward the driver. "Is this enough to cover the trip and a tip?"

The driver wrinkled her nose and gently pushed my hand away. "Don't worry about it, babes. I was headed home, and this was pretty much on my way."

She was lying. This hadn't been on her way home, but the unexpected kindness of the gesture had me swallowing hard. I'd gone from being the bane of my burrow, actively hated by most, and ignored by the few who sympathized, to having people care what happened to me.

Seeing that I was struggling to speak, the driver grabbed my hand and gave it a little squeeze. "I can tell you're dealing with some kind of crapstorm. Us girls have to have each other's back!"

This was not the time for me to start falling apart.

"Thank you," I croaked, my throat tight. "Yeah. Things really suck right now."

That was the understatement of a lifetime.

"Here." The driver scribbled something on the back of a receipt and handed it to me. "That's my number. If you ever need anything, call me. And don't worry if it's late, I'll probably be up late studying for my college exams."

I tucked the scrap of paper into my back pocket. "You have no idea how much I appreciate everything."

"*Psh.*" She waved me away. "Enough of that. Go get a good night's sleep. Things will be better in the morning."

I watched as she merged with the traffic and her taillights disappeared, feeling even more alone and hoping against hope that she was right.

When the car was completely out of sight, I stuck my hands in my pockets and trudged down the street, making my way out of the city and toward the mountains in the distance.

I covered my six-mile hike with ease. Having spent most of my life walking or running to avoid being anywhere but home, running in my human form was second nature to me. My trek ended at the shore of a large lake that sat at the foot of two large mountains.

The moon cast its beams across the surface, giving the lake and the surrounding woods an otherworldly glow. I squinted, searching for the lights of Blackberry Burrow, which was nestled in the valley between the two mountains, but the burrow was completely obscured by the thick forest.

If I'd traveled the road directly to the burrow, I would've had to cover nearly 25 miles thanks to the long, narrow lake that made it impossible to access the burrow any other way. But I had a shortcut.

I was going to swim across the lake, significantly cutting down my travel time.

Searching along the shore, I located a pile of rocks that had fallen, providing me with a place to hide my clothing. The last thing I needed was for a human to happen upon my clothes scattered on the shore and call in the police to search the lake for a drowned swimmer.

I kicked off my shoes and quickly pulled my shirt over my head and wiggled out of my jeans. Folding them, along with my undergarments, I tucked them into the hiding place and hoped they'd still be there when I returned. I was pretty sure the police arrested people for walking into a city naked, and that would be my only option if my stash went missing. Swimming with clothing on wasn't an option since I needed to move freely and didn't want to deal with the drag.

Not wanting to waste any more time, I ran lightly across the rocks and dove into the lake, disappearing into the inky water. As I swam, I became one with the water, focusing on nothing but the steady pumping of my muscles as I moved ever closer to the far shore.

The long swim should have exhausted me, but instead, it cleared my mind and released the anxiety from my tight muscles. By the time I pulled myself from the icy water, I felt nothing but determination.

I could do this.

I *would* do this.

There would be no hesitation because I would do whatever I had to in order to save my men.

It was sometime past midnight by the time I crept into the village. I made my way toward a familiar large oak that had fallen years before. Reaching inside, I sighed with relief as my fingers brushed against the Ziploc bag I'd hidden there. I'd stashed several tiny "go kits" around the edge of the burrow land, never knowing when I might have needed one.

Shame rushed through me because I'd never been brave

enough to actually leave. Not until Fletcher had made that decision for me. But I was a different person now. I was stronger, and I was loved. Most importantly, I had something to live for—my mates.

Quickly unzipping the bag, I pulled out the pair of leggings and a tight crop top. While I would have preferred a comfortable baggy cotton shirt, dealing with excess fabric when trying to be stealthy was a bad idea. The last thing I needed was to get hung on a windowsill or give an assailant a handful of fabric to grip and yank me backward.

Slipping on a pair of thin ballet flats, I pulled my hair into a ponytail. Finally, I reached down and picked up the last item; a large hunting knife. I'd heard the phrase "it fits like a glove," but did anything feel as nice as the handle of a weapon that you'd whittled to create the perfect grip?

Violence was something I despised. I prayed I wouldn't need to use the knife that night, but there was a comfort in knowing I was familiar with this blade.

Over the years, desperate to feel a little less vulnerable, I'd spent hours hiding in storage closets and in the woods with a knife. I'd practiced moving with them until the blade became an extension of my arm. I slid the knife back inside the sheath, and tucked it in the tight band of my leggings, feeling the cool leather press against my skin.

It was game time.

Without a sound, I made my way down the dirt path, blending with the shadows cast by the towering forest as I headed toward the house of a man I'd hoped never to see again. It didn't take long before I was creeping around the red brick house, searching for any sign the man was awake, as well as hunting for the best entry point. The house was dark; not a single light was shining in any of the windows —at least until I reached the back of the house.

There, going up on tiptoes, I peeked into the first-floor room. A tiny reading light was on in his bedroom, providing just enough illumination to see the man. He was sitting in a recliner across from a large bed.

His chin rested against his chest, and a pair of thick-rimmed glasses had slid down until they clung precariously to the tip of his nose. Even through the glass, I could hear his snores. If he sucked any harder, I was pretty sure he was going to peel the wallpaper from the walls. It was a sound that had kept me awake countless nights when he'd visited women in the rooms nearest mine.

Now that I knew which room he was in, it made my decision on where to enter much easier. I made my way back to the front of the house, where I'd noticed a small window above the sink. It had been left slightly ajar, as though he'd intended to close it, but hadn't pushed it all the way down.

Or maybe he'd burned something and was letting in a bit of fresh air? That seemed more likely, since as far as I'd been able to tell, there wasn't a man in the burrow who knew how to cook. Why would they bother to learn when that was a woman's job?

Gritting my teeth, I lifted the window, opening it one slow inch at a time. I crossed my fingers and toes, hoping it wouldn't let out a screech of protest. To my relief, it didn't.

Thanks to my small stature and lack of proper nutrition, I didn't have to lift it very far before I was able to slip inside. I balanced myself over a sink filled with dirty dishes, probably looking like one of those huge Australian spiders.

The stench of days' old food wafted through the kitchen, and I fought the urge to gag. He clearly couldn't cook, but did the man not know how to clean, either? I'd heard the rabbit shifters cracking jokes about how stupid mutt shifters were, but at least my wolf mates knew their way around a kitchen.

Knowing where his bedroom was located made my job easier, and I made my way down the maze of hallways toward the back of the house. I crept into the room, careful not to wake him.

I looked around at the beautifully decorated room. Even in the dim light, I could tell that every piece of antique furniture and art was expensive. It was a stark contrast to the bareness of the women's rooms, which were more of a military dorm room than a home.

Fighting to suppress my sudden annoyance, I moved silently across the thick carpet. For a moment, I longed to lead an uprising against the men of Blackberry Burrow and demand that the women be treated fairly. Then I remembered how terribly it had gone for me the last time I'd taken a stand, and the desire was quickly squashed.

Right now, the best thing I could do for the women of my burrow was to prove that it was possible to escape and remain out of the council's clutches. Maybe then they'd be willing to speak up for themselves. Despite what I'd gone through, I believed change was possible, but it was likely to be slow to come.

Pushing aside my momentary distraction, I stepped behind his chair. I unsheathed the knife and pressed the cool steel against his throat.

With my lips beside his ear, I hissed, "Wake up, old man."

Chapter
EIGHTEEN

CHARLEE

The councilman jerked awake, yelping as the sudden movement caused the blade to press harder against his skin. "What? Who's there?"

I wish I'd prepared a cool response, but I'd been a little too focused on the *getting-answers-and-not-dying* plan to come up with witty dialog. "It doesn't matter. I know the council is controlling the coyotes and that the burrow created a toxin to attack wolf shifters."

"I don't know what you're talking about!" He was careful to keep his body rigid, so the blade didn't dig deeper.

"Shut up! I don't have time to waste with your lies," I snapped. "We're going to keep this short and sweet. Give me the answers I want, and I'll be gone. No one needs to know about my visit or what you told me. How did you poison the wolves?"

"Honestly, I think that information is too difficult for you to understand," he protested, clearly stalling for time.

The fingers of his left hand were creeping toward a pocket on the side of the chair. Was he going for a phone or a weapon? Keeping the knife firmly against his neck, I leaned forward over the chair until I could slip my fingers in the pocket.

"I don't think so," I snarled, pulling out the slim device and shoving it into the pocket on the side of my thigh. Thank goodness these yoga pants had pockets. Why anyone thought pocket-less yoga pants was a good idea, I'd never know.

The councilman moved faster than I'd expected, grabbing my wrist and giving it a hard twist. Biting my lip, I barely kept from crying out. The last thing I wanted was to give him the pleasure of knowing he'd caused me pain.

I let the knife slide against his skin, leaving a long, thin line of blood. "Careful. The next time, you may end up needing stitches."

"You're hurting me!" he whimpered.

"Do you hear that?" I tilted my head, pretending to listen to something. "Oh yeah. It's the sound of me not caring. How did you poison my wolves?"

I realized my mistake too late.

"Charlee!" He spat my name as though it were something gross in his mouth. "Couldn't stay away, I see."

"I would have happily stayed away," I snarled, "but it seems the burrow will not let me go."

"Because you belong to us." Each word was filled with venom and absolute conviction.

"I belong to myself. No man has the right to take that from me."

He had the nerve to chuckle. "We both know that's not true. For such an independent little rabbit, you sure were quick to let those mutts get their paws all over you."

"Don't talk about them like that!" For the first time since arriving in the burrow, my hand shook.

He instantly seized on the sign of weakness. "That's why you're here, isn't it? Those pathetic dogs are dying, aren't they? Or are they already dead? How long has it been since they started showing signs of exposure?"

"Last night."

He barked out a harsh laugh. "Then, by my calculations, they should have died around sunrise."

"They're still alive." I pressed the knife tighter into the fat roll around his neck.

Every fiber of my being wanted to make him pay for his cruelty, but I needed to control my rage before my emotions made me do something I'd regret.

He shook his head, then stiffened, remembering the blade. "Impossible! That toxin is deadly. The wolves we have tested it on lasted less than eight hours. One wolf made it to twelve hours, but he was the strongest of the test subjects."

They'd killed wolves? I swallowed back the bile rising in my throat. Where had the burrow's test subjects come from? I'd known for most of my life that the council comprised monsters, but I hadn't realized just how far they would go to preserve their way of life.

"My mates are still alive, and you're going to tell me how to counteract the toxin," I demanded, proud my voice didn't shake.

"How should I know?" He huffed. "We never wanted to reverse the effects. Every wolf shifter we kill makes the world a better place."

"No! You're lying!" I shrieked, unable to bear the thought of a future without Linc and Copeland in it.

The council had to have an antidote. What if one of the coyotes was accidentally exposed? Even if they didn't care about their hired henchmen, the council was greedy. Surely they'd want an antidote they could use as a bargaining chip if the werewolves threatened their way of life? Like a *hey-we'll-cure-you-if-you-turn-a-blind-eye-to-all-the-creepiness-going-on-around-here* type of thing.

"Dear, I'm retired now. Occasionally, I'll read the lab report. But I much prefer to spend my valuable time discussing issues with the rest of the council and providing companionship for the females." The smugness in his voice made me want to gag.

I doubted there was a single female in the burrows who wanted this creep's companionship. They say there is someone out there for everyone. For him, it was a therapist.

"The wolves have done nothing to you or anyone else in the burrow!" I gritted out between clenched teeth. "They don't deserve to be hurt."

"You belong to us, and by not sending you back, those

flea-bitten mongrels interfered in matters that didn't concern them. If you'd been a good girl, none of this would have happened. So honestly, their deaths are your fault, not ours." His tone was that of a teacher disappointed in a troublesome student.

"No! You sent coyotes onto pack land and purposely set fires! Then you somehow left a toxin meant to kill my mates. I had nothing to do with this evilness!"

"Charlee, Charlee, Charlee." The councilman clicked his tongue. "Those are the consequences of your actions. The wolves are collateral damage. But now you've learned a valuable lesson. We always win." Leaning his head back against the chair, he laughed.

He was far too comfortable for a man with a knife to his throat. "You're an arrogant prick."

"I have every right to be. Haven't you realized we're always going to be two steps ahead of you?" His condescending tone grated on my frayed nerves.

"You're going to give me the reports," I demanded. "And I want every single file the burrow has on this toxin."

"That's not going to happen," he snorted. "Those files are all kept in the lab. And I only get summary reports on my computer at my office in the council building. So, I'm afraid you're out of luck. Checkmate, sweetheart." His sneer of victory caused something to snap inside me.

He thought I would curl up and cry, but he hadn't counted on one thing: the all-consuming power of my desperation. I'd come this far, and I wasn't leaving without the information I needed. Either I got those files or I'd die trying. This made me far more dangerous than he could've ever suspected.

"Get up." My words were low, but something in my tone had him hurrying to comply without protest. "We're going to the lab."

"Are you crazy?"

I shrugged. "Maybe."

"Charlee, even if I let you into the lab, you'll be arrested before you can escape. There's no chance you'll leave with your precious information, so what is the point of this?"

"Enough talking. Start walking." I moved behind him, pressing the knife against the inside of his upper arm.

It was an unusual choice, but the one that gave me the highest odds of taking him out if he fought me. Threatening a victim with a knife to their neck seemed to be the go-to move, but the man was taller than me, and keeping the knife in position was too risky.

"If you move, I'll slice open your brachial artery, and you'll bleed out so fast that not even your healing abilities as a shifter will save you. I'll escape, and you'll be dead before you can call for help or alert anyone to my presence. So, I suggest you move nice and steady. I'd hate to nick you if you make any sudden moves."

I could tell he wasn't sure if he should believe me or not, but thankfully, he was unwilling to take the gamble. He complied, walking slowly down the hall and through the kitchen. As we passed the beautiful cherry-oak knife block, I grabbed another knife that I could press to his back for a little added control.

"Where are your zip ties?" I asked.

"I don't have any—" he began, but immediately shut up when I started yanking open drawers.

Everyone has a kitchen junk drawer filled with all the things you never saw together in any other place—except possibly in a serial killer's murder and torture bag. His was the third drawer I opened. Duct tape, super glue, thumb-tacks, rubber bands, various bits of cord and string, a pair of yellow kitchen gloves, as well as non-threatening items like used batteries, paperclips, old ink pens, and scraps of aging paper. In the back, I found thick black zip ties.

"Put your hands behind your back," I ordered, bracing for him to fight me.

To my immense relief, he obeyed without argument. It was awkward with only one free hand, but with a bit of fumbling and the help of my teeth, I got the zip tie pulled tight. Deciding I might need them later, I tucked a couple more ties, as well as the roll of black duct tape, into my bra.

The medical building that housed the lab was less than half a mile from his home, which we could walk rather than take a car, and risk catching the attention of any guards from the headlights or sound of the engine when we arrived.

It wasn't a hard walk; nevertheless, by the time we reached the side door, he was sweating as though he'd been the one who'd swam a lake. If we'd been natural rabbits and predators had attacked, this plump man would've been one of the first to get eaten.

We stopped in front of the door, and going up on tiptoe,

I whispered near the back of his neck, "You're going to let us in with no fuss and without triggering any alarms. If you do anything stupid to draw attention to us, I will kill you before they get here."

I cut the zip tie and waited. But despite my threat, the stubborn man remained motionless, making no move to type in the code.

My patience was running thin. Every minute he wasted was a minute closer to me losing my wolf mates forever.

"Choose your next move wisely. You can sacrifice your life and protect the burrow's secrets by alerting the guards, or you can be a good boy and open this door with no tricks or chaos." I gave him a shove toward the door. "Unlike the conniving liars that comprise the council, I keep my word. Give me what I want, and I'll let you live."

With his life on the line, the councilman was no longer in the mood to play hero. Stepping closer, he tapped in the code, then pressed his thumb to the fingerprint scanner beside it.

I held my breath, waiting for alarms to blare, but the only sound was the soft click of the bolt clicking and a hiss as the door slid open.

So far, so good, I thought to myself.

We stepped inside. "Where do we need to go? The sooner I get the information, the sooner you'll be free of me."

His shoulders tensed, but then he sighed. "Most of the files are in the record room. Down the hall, third door on the right."

IT'S KIND OF A BUNNY STORY

"Let's go." I pushed him in front of me, keeping my knife between the inside of his arm and his side.

He led the way down the hall and toward the record room, pausing just long enough to type in another code to unlock that door. When we stepped inside, I was relieved to find a bank of computers against one wall and filing cabinets against the opposite. It looked like the type of place where you'd find answers.

But it didn't take long for me to realize I had another problem. I could zip-tie his wrists again, but how could I focus on searching for the information I needed while keeping a man twice my size under control? The moment I was distracted, he'd attack.

Searching the room, I spotted an office chair rolled under a desk. "Sit."

He did as I commanded. Moving behind him, I pressed the knife to his neck. "Put your arms behind your back."

He did, and I zip-tied his wrists a second time, pleased to see I was getting faster. With a little more practice, I could probably be an expert at abducting people.

Pulling the roll of tape from my top, I moved in front of him and began wrapping it around his chest and the back of the chair. As I leaned closer, struggling to reach it thanks to his significant girth, the councilman lifted one of his legs.

Using his thigh, he knocked me off balance so that I fell onto him. Before I could react, he buried his face against my breasts and rocked his hips upward, letting me feel his less-than-impressive erection.

I scrambled away from him. "What is wrong with you?"

183

"You belong to me! Why did you ruin everything, you selfish brat?" His face had turned a strange maroon hue, and his breathing was coming in ragged gasps.

Was he angry, turned on, or having a heart attack?

Please be the latter, I begged the universe.

Not feeding into his tantrum, I began wrapping the tape around his legs.

The councilman wasn't done. "I'd already filled out the paperwork. When your heat started, I was going to have my way with you."

I paused, raising an eyebrow. "With what? That baby carrot in your pants?"

"How dare you speak to me like that, little girl!" he roared.

Ignoring him, I finished taping him to the chair. I used the entire roll, not wanting to risk him working himself free while I searched through the records.

"This is overkill," he snarled.

I couldn't help but notice he resembled a cocoon a beautiful butterfly was preparing to burst free from, except he was more of a slimy worm, and he wouldn't be going anywhere. "It's perfect. Now, stop talking before I decide to cover your mouth... and possibly your nose, too. Hurting you is the last thing I want to do, but it's on the list if I don't get what I want."

Chapter NINETEEN

CHARLEE

"Where are the records?" Leaning down, I held the knife to his throat. "And you better not waste my time! Because if you think I'm short, you should see my patience."

"I told you, I wouldn't know." The man was as arrogant as he was stubborn.

"Then who would know?" I pressed the tip of the knife until he winced.

"Probably the lab rat, Boom... or Boone? Something like that. He's always working on his little side projects in his off time. Personally, I think his research is a waste of the burrow's resources. After all, if a rabbit wants to be disobedient and go against the laws of nature, she deserves whatever comes to her, as does any wolf shifter who tries to interfere. Why should we save them from their own foolishness?" The councilman was far too calm for someone about to face death.

After all, my mates had told me that I needed to kill people. Well, technically they wanted me to keep my stress levels down. But since he was the one causing my stress, it was pretty much the same thing, right?

"And where will I find him?" I snarled.

As if on cue, the office door swung open.

"Councilman, I didn't realize you were going to be in so late."

I kept the knife to the councilman's throat, but nearly snapped my neck when I twisted around to look toward the door. A young man had stepped into the room and froze.

His eyes widened behind thick-rimmed glasses. "I-I will come back later." He stammered, spinning on his heel.

The guy bolted for the door, but I was on him like a tick on a hound dog. I collided with him, knocking him to the ground and grinding my knee into his lower back.

All three of my mates could have tossed me off as though I weighed nothing more than a dust bunny. But he had the tall, lanky build of a man who spent more time indoors than out, which was probably the only reason I kept him pinned. Or maybe he was just too shocked at the sudden change of altitude and plans to do more than lie there with his cheek pressed to the floor.

"Ah, Boone. Just the guy I was hoping to find." My delighted relief at not having to hunt him down gave my voice an unintentional psycho vibe that creeped me out... and if his shiver was any indication, I wasn't the only one.

"Really? You were?" he asked, voice cracking.

"Boone! Do not tell her anything!" the councilman snarled, yanking at the bindings, holding him to the chair. "That is an order!"

"Shut up!" I pointed the knife in his direction, waving it like a teacher wiggling her finger at a naughty student. "Before I make myself a pair of earrings out of your testicles." Not wanting him to believe I'd actually wear them, I added, "And then I'll pierce your ears and make you wear them!"

The councilman's purple face took on a greenish hue, and he snapped his mouth shut.

"I'd like to keep my testicles, if it's all the same to you," the man beneath me wheezed. "I'm Dr. Boone. Happy to make your acquaintance."

I stared at the man beneath me, tilting my head as I studied him. Was he seriously introducing himself to me right now? I hadn't exactly had the chance to do much socializing while living in Blackberry Burrow, or after I left, but even I knew his formality, given the situation, was strange. Was it possible I'd met someone more awkward than me when it came to 'peopling' skills?

Shaking my head, I got back on task. "I'm looking for records regarding the toxin. The one that was formulated by the burrow as a protection against predators."

"Ah, yes. I know what you're talking about."

It seemed he was completely willing to skip the whole *I-don't-have-the-information-you-want* part and get right down to business.

That worked for me.

"Good. I want a copy of every document on that toxin." Deciding he might respond better to niceties rather than threats, I moved from his back, but kept the knife at the ready. "But most importantly, I want to know if there's an antidote."

Boone kept his eyes locked with mine as he pushed himself into a sitting position. He was careful to keep his movements slow and non-threatening.

Smart man. My nerves were shot, and my energy was quickly waning. If he attacked, I wouldn't have the strength to subdue him. I'd have to go for the kill, and I really wanted to avoid that.

"The records aren't a problem. I can copy the entire folder onto a USB drive. But the antidote is... well, that's a problem."

"But there *is* an antidote? Why is that a problem?" I demanded, my rising fears causing it to come out sharper than I'd intended.

Boone flinched, then pushed his glasses up his nose. "Because it's in the early stages of development, and those tests haven't had promising results."

I bit my lip, blinking hard while trying to hold back my tears of frustration. This couldn't be the end. There had to be something I could do other than sit and watch my mates die.

"Let's go to the lab and get the records. I'll explain more as we walk, since you're probably in a hurry to get out of here." Boone's tone was far too gentle for someone who was having his life threatened.

The councilman deserved everything I'd dished out on him, but Boone seemed like a genuinely nice guy. Guilt mixed with my fear and sorrow. Still, I had to finish my mission.

Forcing my emotions to the back of my mind, I glanced between Boone and the councilman, trying to think through my next decision. Boone could be taking me into a trap. But even if that was the case, what choice did I have?

I rose to my feet and hurried to the councilman's side. Grabbing the roll of duct tape, I wrapped it not only around his mouth but also around the back of his head. He might eventually work it off his mouth, but it was going to take him a while. Hopefully that would give me the time I needed to make my getaway.

With a last look back at the duct tape mummy, I followed Boone into the hall. I braced myself, expecting him to grab me the moment I stepped around the corner, but he didn't. Instead, he reached into his pocket and wrote *Fumigation in Progress. Do Not Enter* onto the dry erase board framed on the wall next to the door.

"That should keep anyone from opening the door and accidentally finding him... at least for a little while." He gave me a tentative smile, then ducked his head and hurried further down the hall and away from the entrance where I'd come in. "Okay, so you want to know about the antidote?"

"Yes," I gasped, jogging to keep up with his long-legged strides.

"We've found that all the rabbits living in the burrow have antibodies against the toxin in their blood. This is because of the high levels they are exposed to on a daily basis from the barrier, as well as the plants we grow. We extract the base toxin from parts of those plants, but other parts are edible, and they're used in the kitchens."

"Anything to save money so the council can get richer," I murmured, not even a little surprised.

Boone stopped in front of another door and typed in a code. When the lock clicked, he motioned me inside. "I used blood samples from myself and gave them to the wolves that were exposed to the toxin. The wolves' immune systems responded to the antibodies, but not fast enough."

He sagged down into a well-worn office chair. Removing his glasses with one hand, he pinched the bridge of his nose with the other. "I wanted to save them. Instead, I just prolonged their death."

Staring at the broken young man in front of me, I wanted to rage at him for taking part in what was done to the wolves. But I couldn't shake the feeling that, like me, free will wasn't something he'd been allowed to possess.

"I will save my wolves. Failure is not an option." Straightening my spine, I lifted my chin.

"Your wolves?" Boone's head snapped up, his eyebrows drawing together.

"Two of my mates are wolf shifters, and they've been

exposed to the toxin. It's been over twenty-four hours, and they are still alive."

"That doesn't make any sense." Boone drummed his fingers on the desktop and his gaze took on a faraway look. "None of the wolves survived that long."

Maybe not to him, but I was beginning to connect at least a few of the dots. "I think it might be because they claimed me."

"And by claiming... you mean?" Boone dragged out the question, obviously unfamiliar with werewolf mating behavior.

"Bit me. Left their mark on my neck. Claimed me as their mate." Turning my neck from side to side, I let him see the pale white scars.

"Are you sure they weren't just hungry?" His eyes widened with obvious horror.

"Of course I'm sure," I snorted, then blushed as I remembered what they'd been doing when they'd marked me. "What I'm trying to say is that they ingested some of my blood prior to their exposure."

Boone's confusion gave way to an expression of excitement. "So, they already had some antibodies to the toxin in their system... giving them a leg up when they became exposed."

"Is it possible?" I asked.

"It has to be!" Boone spun in his chair to tap his keyboard and bring his laptop to life. His fingers danced across the keys, blurring as he pulled up record after record. "Yes, that's the only thing that makes sense. We never tried to introduce the antibodies before the exposure, only afterward. And by then, it was too late to do more than delay the inevitable."

"So, what you're saying is my guys have a fighting chance?" My voice shook.

If he hadn't already figured it out, now he knew my mates were my biggest weakness... what I cared about more than anything else on earth. It was something he'd be able to use against me, but there was nothing I could do about that at this point.

I'd moved to stand next to him so I could read the screen over his shoulder. He paused to look up at me. "Yes. As long as they're still alive, there's a chance. But how bad are they?"

"Not good." Exhausted, I sank into the chair next to him.

I kept the knife pointed at him, although I wasn't really worried he was going to try something. He seemed too dedicated to his research, too focused on gleaning information from whatever source he could, to be interested in overpowering me. Other than Fletcher, Boone was the only male rabbit shifter who didn't give off completely icky vibes.

"What if they got more of my blood? Could that save them?" My words came out as barely more than a whisper.

Boone leaned back in his chair. "I don't know. This is uncharted territory."

"But based on your research so far, what's your best guess?" I pressed.

"I don't think your blood possesses enough antibodies. Even if you still lived in the burrow, your antibodies wouldn't be high enough." He paused, then asked. "I'm assuming you're Charlee, the female who managed to get away?"

"Yes." I leveled my gaze at him and lifted my chin, prepared to defend my actions.

Boone gave me a small smile. "Good for you."

Chapter TWENTY

CHARLEE

Based on my past experience with the men in the burrow, I'd braced myself for a nasty remark or a self-important lecture on how I'd done the burrow wrong by stealing their valuable property—and by property, I meant me.

Good for you.

My utter shock at his words stole the very air from my lungs, making it impossible to do more than gape at him.

"I wouldn't blame any of the women for trying to leave." He released a long sigh. "Honestly, they should get away from here. Heck, I'd leave if I could."

"So why don't you?" I asked, genuinely curious. "If the council's ways disgust you, why are you willing to stay and do their dirty work?"

"Don't look at me like that, Charlee." Boone turned away and stared at the laptop screen. "I wasn't the one who started this research. It began long before I was even old enough to work in the lab. My mistake was catching the council's attention by showing 'promise' in mathematics and science in high school. They wanted me in the lab, and they decided on my future career path."

"You could've left," I pointed out. "Men are given more freedom than women; surely you didn't have to stay."

"I know, and I had a whole plan figured out." Boone nodded. "On the outside, I'd nod my head and agree with the council's orders long enough to get my college degree, and then I'd disappear. It worked perfectly... until my last year at the university. That's when the burrow decided to give me a behind-the-scenes tour of their lab, and show me what I'd be working on."

"Seriously? You expect me to believe you didn't know about the toxin until then?" I scoffed, struggling to believe his story.

Boone shrugged. "I can't make you believe anything I say. In fact, you probably shouldn't believe anything someone in the burrow tells you. The council knew what would happen if the wolf packs found out about the toxin, so they weren't willing to risk telling me until they were sure I hadn't gone to university and run my mouth about the burrow's business. When I didn't stir up trouble, they decided I was trustworthy, and it was time to let me in on their dirty secret."

He fell quiet, and the only sound in the room was the soft tapping of his fingers on the keys. Boone was concentrating so hard on his screen that I remained silent. As curious as I was about his backstory, I wanted the documents on the toxin more. My mates were my priority.

After two minutes, he spoke again. "My carefully built plan came crashing down the moment I learned the burrow had created a toxin that could be weaponized. In theory, it could wipe out unsuspecting wolf packs. Not just the paranormal kind, but also the natural predators."

Boone paused to stick a USB drive into the side of his laptop, then continued. "The burrow has a toxin that could destroy multiple shifter species and natural fauna, yet they'd done no research into counteracting its effects. They'd already proven they were willing to use it to kill the wolf shifters they captured. That's why I stayed. By remaining here, I have unlimited access to the toxin and the lab equipment I need for my research. I've dedicated my life and freedom to finding an antidote—and then getting it into the hands of the wolf packs."

I looked at Boone through different eyes. This man wasn't an evil scientist, like I'd assumed everyone in the lab had to be. Maybe there were a few good people in the burrow after all; rabbit shifters who hadn't been wooed by their greed and lust. In a way, Boone had been used and trapped, just as I had been before my escape.

As sad as I was for him, this wasn't the time to let my emotions get the best of me. "So when rabbits are exposed to the toxin, we have a spike of antibodies in our blood. Correct?"

Boone nodded. "Yes, that's right. Any exposure to the toxin causes it. Through the skin or ingestion."

I spun the knife in my hand, a nervous habit. "So, what if I go roll in the plants and expose myself to create a spike?"

He hesitated, then shook his head. "It wouldn't be enough. Your immune system is used to fighting the toxin. So yes, there'd be a spike, but not enough to create the type of antibody load we need if we're going to save your mates."

"Okay, what if you inject me directly with the toxin? Instead of a safe dose, give me several vials of the toxin. I don't care. You could inject me with all of it!"

"No!" Boone spun to face me, his eyes filled with horror. "While a rabbit's body can tolerate exposure to the toxin and you have some antibodies in your blood, your body wouldn't be prepared or able to handle an injection of the toxin in its most potent form."

"But it would cause a spike, right?" I was a bulldog with a bone, one I wasn't ready to release anytime soon.

"Well, yes..." he reluctantly agreed. "It would cause a massive antibody response. But it would have fatal, or at least near fatal, effects."

I took less than ten seconds to absorb what he was telling me. It might kill me, but all that mattered was knowing I had a chance to save my mates' lives if I could get my antibodies to an insanely high amount.

"How long would I have once you've injected me?" I asked, moving to stand over his shoulder again.

"It's not something we've studied." Boone removed his

glasses and rubbed his eyes. "I'm not even sure what a lethal dose of the toxin would be for a rabbit shifter. For all we know, you could be dead within an hour of the injections."

"I understand. All I want is an educated guess," I pressed.

He slid his glasses back on and turned to stare up at me. "If you injected yourself at the levels high enough to make yourself sick and stimulate your immune system, I'd say you had a matter of a few hours before you're unconscious. And I don't know if you'd come out of it, even with medical intervention."

A few hours.

I mentally ran through my escape plan and return journey to the hospital. It would be cutting it incredibly close, but I could work with that.

But there was a chance I'd react badly and die before I made it back to the hospital. Which meant I couldn't risk the information on the toxin dying with me. Regardless of whether I lived or died, the pack needed this information to prepare itself for any future attacks from the burrow.

Moving fast, I press the knife against his neck. "Okay, here's what you're going to do. I want every record, every file, every note, every freaking doodle sent to Bradford Hospital's email."

"Is the knife really necessary?" he grumbled, typing *Bradford Hospital* into his search engine.

"Yes, because I'm asking you to breach security, and I can't risk you fighting me on it." I glanced down to make sure I wasn't actually hurting him. "Besides, if anyone reviews the security tape, you'll have an excuse."

He mumbled something under his breath, but clicked open the hospital's website to a page showing the departments and staff. "Alright, who do you want me to send it to?"

Boone scrolled down the page, but I didn't recognize any of the faces. I racked my brain trying to remember the name the helicopter medical staff had mentioned. "Blaine! Send it to Dr. Blaine!"

"Okay, then." His fingers blurred across the keyboard as he created a new email and typed a quick note.

"I need you to add a note at the bottom. From me," I added before he could hit send.

"Alright." He waited.

I took a deep breath. "To my mates, Fletcher, Copeland, and Linc, I want you to know that no matter what happens, my time spent with you has been the best of my life. To Monroe and Cillian, I'm sorry for the trouble I caused the pack. Please accept this research as a token of my appreciation and apology. I hope it'll help save lives in the future."

"Is that all?" Boone asked, moving the cursor to the send button.

"Yes. Did you attach everything?"

"You have a knife to my neck; of course. I attached a zip folder. I also included a private link to a cloud service where I've hidden away copies of all the research."

"Are you allowed to do that?" I asked.

He laughed. "No, of course not. But after giving up my

hope for a normal future, I wasn't going to risk being cut out from my own research if something were to happen or they were to fire me. It's my insurance policy."

"Okay." I nodded. "Send it."

He sent the email and then slowly turned to me, ignoring the knife mere centimeters from his neck. "We should probably hurry if you're intent on doing this. I'm not positive, but I suspect the council might be monitoring the lab's computer activity. If that's the case, it won't be long before they realize an email with a large file was sent."

"Lead the way." I pulled the knife away from his neck and stepped behind him.

Not wanting to risk accidentally hurting him, I pressed my fingernail against his lower back, letting him believe the knife was still there as an incentive to not test me. As much as I appreciated his openness, I couldn't risk him double-crossing me last minute.

He led us down another long hallway toward a glass-enclosed room. "In here." He jerked his chin toward a door at the far side.

Boone typed in a code to unlock the door, and we stepped inside. Microscopes and elaborate displays of vials and beakers of every size and shape imaginable lined the walls. Cool, sterile air that smelled of disinfectant burned my nose. The scent reminded me of the hospital and the moment I'd turned and walked away from my mates.

For the millionth time, I wondered if they were still alive. They had to be. I'd know if they died, wouldn't I? The pain of being away from them was bad enough. I was sure their death would be unbearable.

"Sit while I prepare the injections." Boone motioned toward one of the padded stools.

He moved into a small, temperature-controlled room. It didn't take him long to return with a tray of tiny vials filled with a purple liquid.

"Aren't injections normally more clear-ish?" I asked, eyeing the liquid warily.

"Is anything ever normal when it comes to the paranormal world?" He gave me a soft smile. "Are you sure about this?" He stuck a needle into one vial and drew the liquid into the syringe. "Charlee, there's no going back if you change your mind. And since no one has been injected with the toxin, there's nothing I can give you if you start going downhill."

"Got it. I'm a guinea pig—or rabbit, in this situation. Since I'm a rabbit shifter, isn't this a type of animal testing?" I teased, trying to put both our nerves at ease.

Boone's dry laugh held no humor. "Do you want it in your arm or your leg?"

"Is it going to make me sore?" I asked.

"That's very likely."

"Then let's do my arm. I need to get out of here as soon as you inject me, and that might be difficult if I can't walk."

Boone leaned toward me, then paused, staring at my arm. I didn't need to be a mind reader to see he didn't want to inject me.

"Listen, you don't have to do this. You've probably

taken an oath or something to not harm people. I can do this myself," I offered, holding out my hand for him to give me the syringe.

Boone drew in a deep breath. "No. If you're determined to do this, I'd rather make sure it's done correctly."

"Thanks. I appreciate that." That I felt relieved was an understatement.

I talked a good game. But realistically, I didn't know if I had the guts to stab myself with a needle... let alone multiple needles.

Unable to help myself, I winced as he jabbed my arm.

Neither of us spoke as he prepared a second injection. He'd just pushed the syringe's plunger on the third when the silence was broken by tires screeching and car doors thudding outside.

Boone rushed to a monitor in the corner and pulled up footage from a security camera out front. "Time's up. You've got to go before—"

Blaring alarms cut off the rest of his sentence. My ears ached from the wailing screech that bounced off the walls and made it impossible to think.

"Charlee, come on!" Grabbing the arm he hadn't jabbed with needles, Boone practically hauled me toward a small side door in the lab.

"Where are we going?" I shouted, barely remembering to hang onto the knife's handle.

For all I knew, Boone was leading me straight to the guards. *'Check it out, guys! I caught the missing bunny who's been causing us all these problems.'*

Yep, that would definitely get him a hefty reward.

"There are three entrances into this building. Front, back, and a small loading door where we used to get deliveries. Deliveries are brought through the front now, so no one uses that door. I'm sure they've already blocked off the front and back, but there's a chance they may have forgotten about that side door. Hurry!" He shoved me down a hallway. "Go past the two doors on the left. The storage room is the door on the right at the end of the hall. There are cardboard boxes stacked nearly to the ceiling against the back wall, but there's a small gap behind them. You should be able to fit. That's where the door is."

Before I could even say thank you, he turned and ran in the opposite direction. Trusting Boone's word, I raced down the hall. The loud shouts and boots pounding on the marble floors told me I was cutting it close. Way too close.

Flattening my palms on the door, I half expected it to be locked, but the door swung open and I tumbled inside. The room looked just like Boone had described it, and I darted for the back wall, spurred on by the voices that were growing louder by the second.

Squeezing behind the boxes, I slid my hand along the door, searching for a handle.

"There!" I breathed, my fingers wrapping around the cool steel handle and twisting.

It was locked.

Well, duh, Charlee. Of course they keep it locked.

Sweat beaded across my forehead and slid down my spine. I was sure part of that was from the fear and adrenaline pumping through my veins, but I suspected it was also the first sign of my body responding to the toxin.

Feeling around, I fumbled with the lock, finally managing to twist the rusted metal. The door creaked open a crack before hitting the boxes and refusing to open any wider. But I was tiny, and the gap was plenty big enough for me.

I squeezed through and collapsed onto a gravel pathway. Breathing in the honeysuckle-scented night air, I fought a wave of dizziness as sweat dripped from my chin and nose to splash on the ground. I wanted to curl into a ball and sleep for a thousand years, but I forced myself to stand. This wasn't where my story was going to end.

Searching the landscape to orient myself, I bolted toward the lake in the distance. I had to get there and get across before my body was too weak to swim. It was my only shot at escaping this place.

As I ran, the lake came into view. I kept my gaze fixed on the glinting surface, trying to ignore the erratic beating of my heart and the strange tingling in my fingers and toes.

Why hadn't I thought to ask Boone about the side effects? It didn't matter. Since he'd never directly injected anyone, it was likely he wouldn't have known what to expect, anyway.

Just as my feet touched the pebbled shore, a man's shout came from behind me, causing my heart to nearly leap from my chest.

"Freeze! Stop right there before I shoot!"

Chapter
TWENTY-ONE

CHARLEE

I gnoring the man, I pushed my trembling legs to run faster. I was so close to the lake, and once I hit the water, no one could catch me. Gravel crunched beneath the man's boots as they pounded against the ground behind me.

I pretended I couldn't feel the tightness in my chest or the burning of my lungs, because if I acknowledged it, I'd be forced to recognize how much trouble I was in. Truthfully, even if I made it to the water before being tackled, I was already exhausted and struggling to breathe. How could I make the long swim to the far shore?

The man let out a string of curses, and his thundering steps drew closer.

"Faster, faster, faster," I repeated like a mantra to myself.

"I said stop!" the man ordered.

Yeah, I'd do that... just as soon as mathematicians reached the last digit of pi.

I wove my way through the trees, but just as I ran onto the pebbled shore, his fingertips brushed against my back. He tried to grab me, but wasn't able to get a grip on my skin-tight top.

Yes! Who's your daddy? I screamed in my mind, delighted that planning had helped me outmaneuver him.

Unfortunately, my momentary victory came to a screeching halt when he grabbed my arm. The toxin-filled injections had already affected my muscles, causing them to grow stiff. Thanks to our momentum, the hard yank backward had a scream ripping from my throat.

Pain.

So. Much. Pain.

My knees buckled from the sudden shock of it. I went down hard, but I wasn't ready to give up, especially when I could practically taste the water.

Rolling quickly to my back, I stared up at the man. With zero hesitation, I pulled back my leg and kicked his chuckle nuggets with every bit of force I could muster. He hit the ground harder than I had.

Not waiting around to gloat, I cradled my aching arm against my chest and scrambled to my feet. But before I could take more than a couple of steps, my attacker's fingers wrapped around my ankle like an iron band. He yanked me off balance, sending me toppling face-first onto the stones.

My chin and cheek collided with the ground. A sickening crack that reverberated through my skull followed the impact, and I was pretty sure my brain was bruised from rattling about. Still, I didn't have time to dwell on my injuries. Especially when I had already caught the beam of a flashlight hurrying toward us. The guard's backup had arrived.

Which meant this was my last chance to escape.

Fleeing wasn't going to work, so I was left with only one option.

Yanking the knife from its sheath at my waist, I threw myself toward my would-be captor. He went from being the predator to becoming my prey, and his momentary shock at the role reversal gave me the slight advantage that I needed.

I aimed for his chest. People liked to think that when you stabbed someone, the knife would go in like butter. That wasn't always the case, and things like whether the person was wearing cotton or leather, and where the knife penetrated, could change the outcome. That, combined with our size difference, meant I'd need to put my all in this one attack, because he wouldn't give me a second chance.

It was a kill or be killed situation. And if I was about to be killed, I was taking him with me.

You'd be proud of me, Linc, I thought, throwing all my weight behind the knife.

At the last second, the man jerked his body to the left, causing my blade to slice a line across his chest before plunging into his skin just below his collarbone. While the knife sank deep, it hit nothing vital.

Before I could pull my weapon free, the guard

backhanded me with so much force that I tasted blood. The sudden explosion of white-hot pain lit up the dark night, momentarily blinding me as he shoved me off him. Leaping to his feet, he sent the metal toe of his boot into my stomach.

Unable to breathe and still struggling to see thanks to the brilliant pain lighting up every nerve ending in my body, I could do little more than curl into the fetal position and try to protect myself from another attack. With difficulty, I did my best to push past the agony that was stealing my ability to come up with a plan.

Heck, forget about coming up with a plan! I wasn't sure I remembered how to breathe, let alone problem-solve.

The man's ragged breathing was followed by the metallic click of a gun being cocked.

I forced my eyelids open and stared up at him, letting him see the defiance I felt toward everything in this cursed burrow.

He spat, grinning evilly when it hit my cheek. "If you so much as flex your pinky, the next bullet goes through your brain. You've been nothing but trouble for the burrow. I'd prefer to kill you here and now, but I have a feeling the council is going to want to question you about the wolf pack's inner workings. Although I suspect you'll continue being a disappointing waste of their time."

"And you're a waste of oxygen."

The guard's eyes widened, and he spun around toward the voice.

Boone stood behind him. Stepping back, he lifted his hand to display an empty syringe.

"What did you do?" the guard grunted, muscles in his neck bulging and his mouth wide as he tried to breathe. "What did you inject me with?"

Boone looked at the syringe, then dropped it to the ground as though it burned his fingers. "Something that doesn't have an antidote, I'm afraid."

The guard sagged to the ground, odd, strangled sounds coming from his throat. "What's happening... to... me...?"

"Every muscle in your body is becoming paralyzed. This will make it impossible for your lungs or heart to function." Boone kicked the gun well out of the reach of the dying man.

"What are you doing here?" I asked, my aching brain struggling to comprehend what was happening.

So sure had I been that the approaching flashlight belonged to the guard's backup, I never even considered the possibility that *I* might have had backup.

"You didn't actually think I was going to let you go alone, did you?" He raised a single eyebrow.

"Well, yeah, that's exactly what I thought." I pushed myself into a sitting position. Nausea overwhelmed me, and I twisted around to vomit on the rocks. When I could speak again, I asked, "What about your research and everything you've done here?"

Reaching down, he offered me a hand and helped me to my feet. "The moment I sent that email, I knew my work in the lab had ended. Do you think the council would ever trust me again? Even if I claimed you had a gun to my head and forced me to send the email and steal the toxin, they'd still need someone to blame and make the public scapegoat. Do you really want the guilt of leaving me behind on your conscience?"

He wasn't wrong. I'd ruined his future here at the burrow.

"Hey, don't look so glum, Charlee. This was the kick in the butt I needed to make better decisions. If it makes you feel any better," he added as he looped my arm around his shoulders, "I have to admit, I'm pretty excited to see where this new research goes."

"New research?" Each word was a struggle to get out thanks to the throbbing of my cheek and jaw. "Research? What research?"

"Isn't it obvious? The success rate of a possible antidote on werewolves who've ingested antibodies prior to exposure. Plus, I want to know the effect of injecting such a large dose of the toxin has on our bodies."

"Our bodies?" It was becoming harder to concentrate thanks to the pounding in my head that became louder with each beat of my heart. "Where are you taking us? I have to swim back."

"Lee—can I call you that? I know your name's Charlee, but I figure with us being in a mess together, we could go with nicknames at this point."

"Yeah, sure." My words came out slurred as though I'd had too many shots. It was kind of true. Injections were shots, just the less fun kind.

"You're in no shape to swim and would drown before you made it halfway across. There's no way I'm going to let such a valuable chance to further my research sink to the bottom of the lake." He chuckled. "I've got a car. You can use my cell phone to call the pack. If they've realized you're missing, they're probably already losing their minds. And I'd prefer if you told them about me before they find me in the car with you so I don't end up in a kill-first-ask-questions-later situation. I've heard wolves are pretty protective of their packs."

As hard as I tried, I couldn't get my heavy limbs to obey the commands my brain was giving them. By the time we reached the car, Boone was practically carrying me.

He settled me into the passenger seat, and my head slumped back onto the headrest, too heavy for my neck to continue holding up. My vision had grown so blurry that I couldn't even make out the time on the car's console.

Boone dropped into the driver's seat and put the car in gear. He kept the headlights off as we shot down the gravel road and through the burrow's gated entrance.

"What did you mean when you said *our bodies?*" I pressed the back of my hand against my mouth as nausea rippled through me. What if I vomited in his car after everything he'd done to help me?

"We have no way of knowing how many vials of blood with the antibodies will be needed to save your men. Not to mention, it's possible someone else in your pack could get exposed before an antidote can be figured out." Boone flipped off his headlights as he turned off the gravel drive and onto the paved main road. "So, after I sent you toward the side exit, I went back and injected myself."

"You did what?" My eyes flew open. "Are you crazy? You don't even know my mates!"

"I don't know them. But I'm aware of what the burrow put you through, and they must be pretty amazing for you to step foot inside these boundaries again." Using his sleeve, he wiped at the sweat dripping from his forehead into his eyes. "It's time for change, and I want to be part of that."

"Thank you," I sniffled.

"For possibly killing you by injecting you with a toxin? Or for rescuing you?"

"Both." My laugh was more of a wheeze.

"You're welcome." His fingers tightened around the steering wheel.

"I don't know how I'll ever repay you for this— assuming we both survive." My heartbeat was becoming more erratic, staying on beat about as well as a drunk girl singing karaoke.

Boone shook his head. "You don't owe me anything. In fact, I'd say the council owes all the women in the burrow for what they've put them through."

He turned to me with a cheeky smile. "Although, if either of your wolf mates has a sister who's single, I'd love an introduction. As you're aware, dating isn't a thing in Blackberry Burrow. Even if it were, a lab nerd like me doesn't get out much. It can be lonely."

Was it just me, or was his breathing becoming raspier

with each word he spoke? Boone sneezed once, twice, a third time. "Is it cold in here? I'm going to turn up the heat."

He clicked several buttons on the dash, and warm air began blasting out of the vents. I said nothing because we both knew the truth. We were getting sicker, and our fevers were getting worse.

"Here." Boone held out a cell phone. "Call the pack. I don't think it'll be safe for me to drive us all the way to the hospital. See if they have anyone who can meet us now that we're past the toxic perimeter."

"I don't know anyone's number," I admitted, my fingers tightening around the small device in my hand.

"Huh. That's a problem. It's not like we can Google werewolf pack alpha's numbers," Boone joked, his laugh quickly turning into a cough.

I couldn't help but snort with amusement. If you could simply Google an alpha's number, the man's phone would never stop ringing once the BookTok girlies got ahold of it. They'd never be able to resist a real werewolf.

Shooting Boone a small smile, I tapped the screen. "I have an idea."

"Let's hope it's a good one," Boone teased before succumbing to another round of violent sneezes.

Opening the internet browser, I did a quick search and found the number of the hospital. I called the number, listening to it ring as I waited for someone to answer.

"Bradford Hospital. How may I direct your call?" an elderly-sounding woman answered.

"My ma…" I trailed off, unsure if the woman was a werewolf or a human. "My husband was brought into the hospital a few hours ago. Dr. Blaine is his doctor. Can I speak with one of his nurses to get an update?"

I waited while she transferred the call. Instead of a nurse or the doctor picking up, it was a familiar voice that yelled through the phone, nearly busting my eardrum.

"What hare-brained idea did you come up with?" Monroe demanded. "And don't bother lying because I know you're doing something your mates wouldn't have agreed to if you'd bothered to discuss it with them first. Fletcher thinks you went to Blackberry Burrow, and he's in the process of raising an army to storm its gate. And Linc gained consciousness just long enough to rip out his IVs so he could come after you. They had to give him a double dose of horse tranquilizers to take him down just to get him back in the bed."

"Everything is fine, and I'm safe!" I squeaked out, trying to cut off her tirade.

"For now!" she shot back. "I wouldn't be too sure of your safety once your three men get their hands on you!"

Tears of joy sprang to my eyes, and I sniffed. "They're both still alive?"

Just as quickly as it had come, her frustration with me melted away. "Yes, they are. But you need to hurry back. They're not getting better, and the doctors think it would be best if you were here."

I'd held it together as long as I could, but I'd reached my breaking point, and her words tipped me over the edge. My quiet sniffles turned to great racking sobs that shook my body, making it almost impossible to breathe.

The car jerked as Boone reached over to snatch the phone where it had fallen in my lap. "Hi? I'm Boone, and we're headed your way, but we need help. Do you have anyone you can send to meet us? We think we can save her mates, but I'm not confident I'll be able to get us there safely."

I zoned out as he rattled off directions for a meeting point and hung up. Lost in my exhaustion and the toxin spreading through my veins, I wasn't sure how much time had passed before the car rolled to a stop on the side of the road. Before either of us could react, his door was wrenched open.

"How dare you!" a female snarled before throat-punching Boone and hauling the gagging man out of the car as though he weighed nothing.

The female tossed him on the ground, then leaned down so she could see me. "It's okay. You're safe now." Her eyes glowed just like Linc's and Copeland's eyes.

So she was a wolf shifter.

"I'm Reese, Monroe's best friend," she continued, giving me a friendly smile. "You must be Charlee."

"Did Monroe send you?" Boone choked out the words.

"No, she didn't send me, you barbaric, backwoods, brother-banging, black-hearted, boring buffoon of a bunny!" Reese snarled, trying to kick him, but Boone caught her foot at the last minute.

"Hey, that hurts." He used his free hand to adjust his glasses. "I'm not boring."

It wasn't until that moment that it dawned on me that she was butt-naked. Wolves didn't seem to care much about modesty. Reese yanked her foot free and tackled him, straddling his chest as she prepared to choke the life from him.

"I'm one of the good guys," Boone protested, trying his best to look anywhere but at Reese's bare chest, which was practically shoved in his face. "I spoke to Monroe on the phone, and she was going to have someone meet up and drive us to the hospital."

Reese paused, suspicion written all over her face. "I've been running in my wolf form, idiot. How was she supposed to call me? I haven't exactly been taking phone calls, and I'm too far from the alpha for him to relay a mental message."

Opening my car door, I staggered to my feet. "We think we have something to help my mates, but we have to get to the hospital. Fast. We can sort this mess out later. Can you drive us there?" Using the car as a support, I made my way around to stand beside them.

"I'm happy to drive you there. But him..." She cocked an eyebrow and jerked her chin down to where Boone lay beneath her on the ground. "I'd rather leave him here."

"Boone's a good guy. He saved me, and he wants to help the pack." My legs trembled. I wasn't going to be able to stay standing much longer.

"You're sure you're not a bad bunny?" Reese leaned down and growled in his face.

Instead of being offended, Boone gave her a dopey smile. "I can be if you want me to be."

That earned him a genuine laugh from Reese. "You might be alright. Who knows? Maybe I'll just keep you. Monroe is so adorable, but her mates refuse to let me keep her as a pet."

"You can keep me as long as you want," he promised.

I rolled my eyes. Was he seriously going to fall for the first girl he met?

"This has to be the world's most violent meet-cute ever. I'm going to vomit, and I don't know if it's because of the toxin or all the flirting. Right now, I need Reese to focus and get me to my mates."

"Yes, we need to get you back." Reese's glowing eyes searched the road behind us. "Not to mention it's possible the burrow could've already sent people after you. We need to get back to the hospital, where the pack can protect us."

With that decided, she opened the back seat, grabbed Boone by the collar of his shirt, and tossed him inside. "Let's go."

Chapter
TWENTY-TWO
FLETCHER

The only reason I'd allowed Charlee to board the helicopter without me was my belief that the critical condition of Linc and Copeland would keep her close to them. But I should've known better. Charlee wasn't one to sit around when something needed to happen, and she'd figured out a way it could be done.

She'd never been the type to jump from one half-baked idea to another. Charlee was far too smart for that. But she had zero problems taking a risk, especially if she'd calculated the odds and felt they were in her favor. That meant that if she'd risked everything to go back to Blackberry Burrow, she believed something there could change the outcome of this tragic situation.

I understood why she couldn't take any wolves from the pack—not when there was a deadly toxin involved—but I wished she would have trusted me to go with her. So why had Charlee decided to go alone? Why hadn't she at least told someone?

Because she knew we wouldn't have let her go, or she'd determined success was more likely if she did this herself.

"Shouldn't they be here by now?" I stared through the glass windows of the emergency room. The dark of night was giving way to the soft blues and purples of a sun that hadn't risen but was just beginning to wake.

"They're nearly here." Monroe stood at my side, looking up at me with a sympathetic smile. "Fletcher, we need you to be prepared. Reese just called, and from what she said, Charlee isn't doing well."

Her words caused everything around me to fade away until I no longer heard the beeping of medical machines, the buzzing of fluorescent lights, the crackle of intercom announcements, or the noise of the anxious members of the pack that filled the lobby. The reality that I might lose my mate caused my world to dim. Without her sweetness, my world was bleak and boring.

I'd wanted to give her the world. Since I couldn't do that, I'd risked everything to give Charlee her freedom. All she'd gotten was just over a week of happiness before it had been taken away from her. If I lost her, I knew I should be thankful and cherish that brief window of heaven, but life would be incredibly bitter after getting a taste of what I could never have again. How would I survive losing her?

Headlights came into view, growing larger as a vehicle sped toward the hospital. Without bothering to slow, the car careened into the parking lot on two wheels and screeched to a halt in front of the glass doors. The driver leaped out of the car, not even bothering to turn off the engine.

"Charlee's in the passenger seat." The woman, clad only in a man's dirty dress shirt, let out a string of curses that could make a sailor blush. "Where's the medical team?!"

I beat everyone to the passenger side of the car and yanked open the door. Charlee had curled into a ball, her cheek resting on the console between the seats. Her pale face and small size made her appear more like a sleeping doll rather than a living human.

She was completely motionless, her breathing so shallow that her chest wasn't rising or falling. I reached out, terrified I'd find her skin cool because she'd already left me. But before I could touch her, the medical staff pushed me aside.

They quickly transferred her from the car to a stretcher, then rushed back inside. The staff moved with the speed of a well-oiled team… or shifters who were afraid their alpha would destroy them if they failed to save her. They were taking her directly into Dr. Blaine's private facility, which was off limits to the rest of the hospital, but I still wasn't sure how many members of the staff were paranormal or if some were humans who'd been let in on our secret. That was a rare occurrence because of our need for secrecy, but it would make sense to have some humans working in various hospitals who could alert local alphas when an unconscious paranormal was brought in.

I stumbled into the hospital after them, my legs feeling as though they might give out from the weight of my grief.

As a second stretcher rushed by me, I squinted, trying to focus on the man's face. He looked vaguely familiar.

Monroe appeared at my side and must have read my confused expression. "That's the shifter who helped Charlee escape."

"He's a rabbit shifter?" I asked, still trying to place his face.

"Yes. That's Boone." The wolf who'd driven Charlee to the hospital walked down the hall toward us. She stuck out her hand. "Hi, I'm Reese."

On autopilot, I grasped her hand and shook it. "Fletcher. And thank you for bringing Charlee back to us."

Reese shrugged. "No problem. I wasn't the only one out there searching for her. I just happened to get to them first."

I stared down the hall in the direction they'd taken Boone. My mistrust of the burrow ran deep, and I found it hard to believe one of the men had helped her out of the goodness of his heart.

"Are you sure he's actually here to help?" I asked.

"There are only three things in life you can be sure of. Taxes, death, and needing to pee as soon as you get into bed. But yeah, my gut says Boone's one of the good guys." The way her eyes softened as she spoke made me think her heart was saying some things about him, too.

Interesting. I filed the observation away.

"What happened to him and Charlee?" The image of my mate's bruised face flashed through my mind. "What did the burrow do to her?"

"I don't have all the details since they became incoherent shortly after I found them." Reese ran trembling fingers through her hair. "Apparently, Boone injected Charlee with a high dose of the toxin."

"He did what?" My voice came out sharper than I'd intended, and several pack members' heads snapped in my direction.

They'd accepted me and had treated me with nothing but kindness, but I knew any show of violence would end with me being nothing more than a lucky rabbit's foot on someone's keychain.

Reese waved her hand toward the shifters to let them know she was fine. "Only because she forced him to. He didn't like her plan any more than you do."

"I find that hard to believe. What did she do? Hold a gun to his head? The man is nearly twice her size!" I demanded.

"Not a gun." Reese smirked. "It was a knife, actually."

"You can't be serious." My jaw dropped in disbelief.

"Dead serious." Reese grinned, looking positively delighted at my mate's abilities.

Despite what she said, I struggled to reconcile it with the Charlee I knew. She was such a sweet, gentle person. It was difficult to imagine anyone would feel threatened by her, with or without a knife. It was the equivalent of an adult being scared of a kid with a sharp pencil… Then again, kids could be terrifying. So maybe a pint-sized woman wielding a knife was just as disconcerting.

"That explains what happened to Charlee, but why does

he look like he's on death's doorstep?" I focused back on Reese.

"Because he injected himself with the toxin as well."

My eyebrows shot up. "Why would he do that? It's not his mates who are dying. The men in the burrow don't do things from the kindness of their hearts—they don't have hearts."

"I don't know. Guilt over the part he might have played in this mess? Maybe he was inspired by the courage and love your mate showed. Not many people can face their traumas head-on." Reese bit her lip, seeming to think over what she wanted to say next. "From what I've heard, you treat her as though she's a fragile thing that can easily be broken. But you've got your girl all wrong, and you need to watch out. One misstep on your part, and I'm pretty sure you'll find yourself neutered. The girl's good with a blade, after all."

Her wicked smile had me feeling like I needed to check if my testicles were still intact. But not wanting to show weakness, I resisted and stuck my hands in my pockets instead.

"I think I'm going to go make sure Boone's okay. After all, he doesn't know anyone here except Charlee and me." Reese trotted down the hall.

Yep. There was definitely something going on between the two of them. Monroe and I followed after her. "I'll come with you. They won't let me see Charlee right now." Truthfully, I just didn't want to be alone.

We slipped inside Boone's room, moving to stand

against the wall so we weren't in the doctor or nurses' way. They bustled around his bed, attaching various wires and tubes to him.

The doctor leaned close to Boone, scribbling notes on a pad of paper. Every word the rabbit shifter spoke took tremendous effort, but he was determined to relay as much information to the doctor as possible. It was as though Boone was afraid once he fell unconscious, he'd never wake again, and he didn't want to take this information to the grave.

Despite his determination, the toxin claimed victory over his willpower. His words slurred together until his speech was barely intelligible.

"You've done as much as you can. Now shut up and get some sleep." Reese had wiggled between the nurses to appear next to his bed. Her words were bossy, but the way she tucked the blanket around him and gently squeezed his fingers belied how she felt.

"She's right," the doctor agreed, motioning for the nurses to back away from the bed. "With the information you emailed us, and Charlee's and your sacrifice, I think we have a chance to save the wolves. Now it's time for you to focus on your own survival."

The doctor had an incredible poker face, so I couldn't tell if he was lying or not. But it didn't matter, because his assurance was exactly what Boone needed to hear. With a tired nod, he closed his eyes and allowed unconsciousness to claim him.

I stepped out into the hall, watching as doctors and

nurses hurried past. For the first time since this nightmare had begun, there was an extra bounce in their step and hope in the weary lines of their faces.

So the doctor hadn't been lying. There was a chance.

I just prayed Charlee hadn't given up her life to bring that about.

"What do we do now?" I asked, voice cracking.

Monroe touched my elbow. "I think we should go check on Charlee."

Chapter TWENTY-THREE

FLETCHER

M onroe led me past the hustle and bustle of the staff, and through several doors marked *Employees Only*. We stepped into a small room that was attached to the lab.

"It lacks the privacy of a private room, but being so close allows the doctors to monitor Charlee's vitals while they begin working on a vaccine to give the pack prior to exposure to help lessen the effects of the toxin. They are also working on an antidote that could help those who've been exposed," Monroe explained.

"I prefer having the doctors working within feet of her, rather than having her in a room by herself." It was the truth.

"Cillian told me Linc and Copeland have already received the first transfusions. Now it's a waiting game to see how their bodies respond." Monroe stepped aside and motioned for me to walk ahead of her toward the bed.

Charlee was just as eerily still as she'd been in the car. An IV line ran from her arm into some kind of machine that appeared to be collecting her blood.

Several feet away, doctors rolled between computers and microscopes, frantically typing notes every few minutes. A lab assistant prepared several slides, putting a drop of crimson liquid from one vial onto each thin piece of glass. Task finished, she retrieved a second vial and dripped that liquid on top of the first. Was that Charlee's blood?

Science hadn't been my favorite subject in school, but even an idiot could have figured out the doctors were testing the reactions of wolf shifters' blood to the toxin and the antibodies. When I'd arrived at the hospital several hours after Linc and Copeland had arrived, Dr. Blaine still hadn't known how to save the wolves. The staff could do nothing more than keep the wolf shifters comfortable and hope their bodies could somehow defeat the toxin on their own. A sense of heaviness had hung over the facility, but now, an undercurrent of excitement hummed through the room.

Not bothering to ask for permission, I climbed into bed beside Charlee, tucking her tiny body against mine. I pressed a gentle kiss to her bruised cheek, frustrated that I hadn't been there to protect her when she'd needed me. It was a failure I would have to live with, and I wasn't sure I could ever leave her side again.

For hours, we lay like that. I didn't sleep, and instead

watched the doctors, my heart soaring each time they shoved a chair back in excitement and called the other doctors to examine whatever they were seeing, only to feel it sink when their brows creased with new lines of frustration.

A large screen took up almost the entirety of one wall. Dr. Blaine stood in front of it, studying the burrow's documents on the toxin, and comparing it to the reports being handed to him from the surrounding doctors. They were desperate to glean any information that could help them create an antidote and a vaccine as quickly as possible.

Listening to the medical team talk, I gathered that while a small number of antibodies prior to exposure had kept Linc and Copeland healthy longer than usual, it hadn't been nearly enough to save them. Dr. Blaine wanted to create a vaccine that would last longer in the body, and would amplify the effect of the antibodies without needing to risk rabbit shifter lives in the process.

Honestly, they were attempting to do the impossible. Yet somehow, they pulled it off. And work that should've taken years, they figured out in less than four hours.

"It worked!" Dr. Blaine shouted, shoving away from the microscope. He smacked his palms on the granite counter.

I pushed up in bed, and Monroe lifted her head from where she'd fallen asleep against Cillian's chest.

"You believe you have a working vaccine?" Cillian asked.

The doctor grinned. "Only time will tell, but I'm pretty confident." The doctor grinned. "It will likely require an initial injection, and then follow-up boosters over time, but it should prevent the wolves from being affected by normal exposure to the toxin. Depending on their immune system, it's possible that some wolves may experience symptoms after exposure similar to a cold, but with refinement, we may be able to minimize those cases as well. I'd like to make a small batch to ensure we are correct."

"Do it," Cillian ordered. "And let us know if there's anything we can help you with."

"No. No, I think we have it," Dr. Blaine assured him, rushing to help his team.

Clearing my throat, I interrupted the excited chatter. "What about Linc and Copeland? How are they?" I was terrified to hear his answer.

Dr. Blaine turned to face me, his face grim. "They're still alive. All we can do is wait and hope the transfusions of the antibodies worked."

I fell silent, watching them work to create a small batch of the vaccine. When the team finished, they hurried out of the room with Cillian and Monroe following on their heels. I stayed, refusing to leave Charlee alone. Linc and Copeland were in the best hands possible.

Charlee's breathing was shallow, but steady. She'd sunk into a coma, but the doctor had assured me she was stable and just needed time for her body to heal itself. I found that hard to believe while staring at a face so pale I could see the veins beneath her skin. There was nothing I wanted more than to see her smile at me and look into her big green eyes. Would I see them again?

For nearly an hour, I lay stroking Charlee's hair and counting each beat of her heart. I glanced toward the door as footsteps in the hall grew closer. Dr. Blaine and two nurses came through the doorway and made their way toward us. My stomach sank as I saw their expressions. Something hadn't gone as planned.

"Are they still alive?" How could I bear to face Charlee if she woke to find they were gone?

"It's too soon to know about the vaccine." Dr. Blaine cleared his throat. "As for Copeland and Linc, the transfusion worked, but because of their critical condition, it wasn't enough."

"What does that mean?" I asked.

My unease grew as the doctor and nurses exchanged glances.

"We need more of her blood," Dr. Blaine explained.

They'd been in the process of taking blood from her when I'd arrived in the room, and they hadn't seemed concerned then. "Why are you asking for my permission now?"

The doctor scrubbed a hand down his face, looking grim. "Because we need to take a significant amount of her blood, far more than a safe donor amount. We'll give her a transfusion immediately after, but I won't lie. It's risky."

My arm tightened around her fragile body. "How can you even ask that of me—of her? Charlee has already given too much blood. Hades! She's in a coma because her body is struggling."

He sighed. "We understand, and if there were any other way, we'd try that first. But we're out of time and options."

I refused to do anything that would risk losing her. "What about Boone? I thought he was giving blood as well."

The doctor shook his head. "We're taking as much as we can from him as well. Dr. Boone insisted he wanted us to take as much of his blood as possible rather than weakening Charlee any further. We honored his wishes, but we can't risk taking any more from him, and we were forced to start giving him a blood transfusion."

"Then take mine," I insisted.

"It wouldn't work. You don't have enough of the anti-bodies in your bloodstream. Even if we injected you with the toxin now, it would take a couple of hours before we could start taking your blood." The doctor was patient in his explanations, but he kept checking his phone, seeming more agitated with each notification he received.

Finally, he met my gaze head-on. "Sir, I know you're frustrated, and I'd feel the same if it were my mate. The alpha ordered that the decision is to be left in your hands."

"Then I say absolutely not. We're not putting her life at further risk. She's done more than enough." My tone made it clear this wasn't open for negotiation. "You'll have to find another way."

An older nurse with kind eyes moved to the side of the bed. "Dear, I can't imagine what you're going through, and we will honor your wishes. But right now, you're Charlee's voice. Please take a moment to consider what she'd want."

Tears sprang to my eyes. "I can't lose her."

"And she doesn't want to lose any of you." The nurse gently patted my arm. "Without more of her antibody-rich blood, Linc and Copeland will not make it. Seeing how far she was willing to go to save them, when she wakes up, are you prepared to tell her you made this decision for her?"

I wanted to be angry at the nurse for pushing for me to change my mind, but I couldn't. How could I when she was only speaking the truth?

If I said yes, and Charlee died, I'd lose her. But if I said no, and the wolves died, Charlee would never forgive me, and I'd still lose her. Either way, she'd be gone. As hard as it was, I needed to do what she would have wanted.

I ran my fingers down her silky hair. "Charlee? I need you to be strong. You have a little more work to do." Without looking up, I choked out, "Do it. Save Linc and Copeland."

HOURS LATER, Dr. Blaine dropped into the chair next to the bed. He dropped his head back against the seat and closed his eyes. Charlee was weak, and she remained in a coma, but her vitals had stabilized.

The minutes ticked by, with the doctor remaining silent. Unable to handle the stress of not knowing, I asked, "How are Linc and Copeland?"

"They are finally out of the woods," he responded without opening his eyes. "In the last thirty minutes, we've witnessed signs that their shifter healing abilities are working to repair the damage done to their bodies."

The tension in my muscles relaxed, and I drew in the first full breath I'd taken since this nightmare began.

Opening his eyelids, he met my relieved gaze. "We would have lost them if Charlee hadn't secured the research and injected herself with the toxin. She's a hero."

"I know," I murmured.

Clearing his throat, the doctor continued, "Based on Linc and Copeland's survival, and what we're seeing on the blood drawn from the shifters who volunteered to receive the first doses, I believe we've found the answer to preventing many more deaths. And it requires a lot less blood be taken from Charlee and Boone since we wouldn't be trying to save wolves who were on death's doorstep."

"Will you start on another batch of the vaccine right away?" I asked, still worried about the burrow retaliating.

"No," Dr. Blaine sighed. "We can't until we have more blood to work with."

My jaw dropped. "Are you asking for more of her blood?" There was no disguising the horror in my tone.

"Of course not. Boone and Charlee will be far too weak to give any more blood for quite some time. Which means it's going to be a long while before we can stock the vaccine and begin dosing the pack. And we will need more blood to continue research on an antidote that can be used to save those who are exposed but never received the vaccine."

"They aren't the only rabbit shifters you have at your disposal, Dr. Blaine," I reminded him, holding out my arm. "Take mine and get the work started."

For a moment, he looked excited, but then he frowned. "It's not just rabbit shifter blood that is needed. You'd have to be injected with the toxin. It would be a smaller dose, nothing like the near-fatal levels Boone and Charlee used on themselves. But you'll still feel its effects, probably similar to having a bad case of the flu."

He would not change my mind. "I understand. But knowing how vindictive the Blackberry Burrow is, we need to do whatever we can to protect the pack. We don't have the luxury of sitting around to see if the burrow retaliates."

"Which is why I'm not going to argue with you." The doctor pushed himself out of the chair with a groan. "If you're willing to suffer through the toxin's effect, I'll go tell the nurses to prepare the injection. The sooner we can start this, the sooner we can protect the pack."

A rustle came from the doorway, and we both turned to find Monroe and Ellora.

"Tell the nurses to prepare injections for us as well." Monroe gave me a smile. "Like Fletcher said, Boone and Charlee aren't the only rabbits in the hospital."

The doctor hesitated, his eyebrows drawing together. "Monroe, are you sure about this? Are you sure the alpha is okay with this?" Then his eyes slid to Ellora, and he looked more than a little afraid. "And you've discussed this with Mac?"

I'd yet to meet this Mac guy, but with the way everyone

spoke, you'd have thought he was a villain, not one of the good guys. Was the man truly that intimidating?

"Of course I did!" Ellora laughed. "I wouldn't risk him ripping your head off. Our men aren't exactly happy about it, but they understand why it needs to be done."

"Then, if you're sure, I'm not going to turn down the offer." With that, the doctor hurried out of the room. Even though he was tired, his steps had a bounce in them.

Chapter TWENTY-FOUR

CHARLEE

I'd always wondered what happened after a shifter died. In my case, it appeared I'd taken a trip to the humid stickiness and scorching heat of the South... and I wasn't talking about Florida. Yep. All signs pointed to me having just woken up in Hades.

Well, crap!

I racked my brain trying to figure out what I'd done to earn a spot here. Surely it wasn't because I wanted to kill the councilman? Those had only been thoughts. Maybe it was the stabbing and slashing? Stabbing was bad, right?

No, I was pretty sure I knew what—or who—had gotten me here. It was all my inner bimbo's—I mean, *shifter's*—fault because she only ever had one thing on her mind. I couldn't even be mad, though. I'd wanted my guys just as much. If it was lust that had bought my one-way ticket to become a smoke show, I was willing to accept it.

An incessant beeping somewhere in the distance was growing louder. My head throbbed as though the sound was drilling a hole through my skull.

Carrot top! I'd thought the heat was terrible, but this was way worse. Hell was supposed to be awful, but listening to the repetitive beeping for all eternity was a special type of torture I didn't think I deserved.

I tried to place the sound. Smoke alarm? No, that would've been stupid for hell. And a fire drill would have been redundant. As my annoyance flared, the sadistic beeping grew faster. My groan of frustration was cut short by movement next to me. I'd yet to open my eyes, but clearly, I wasn't alone.

I swear to McGregor's garden, if I open my eyes and find a demon trying to reach me about an extended car warranty...

"She's waking up," a deep, sexy voice rumbled.

Nope. Stop thinking about yummy voices, Charlee. That's what got us here in the first place! I chided my inner floozy.

With supreme effort, I tried to open my eyelids, but they must have been super-glued shut because they didn't budge. How long had I been dead?

"Charlee, come back to us."

Wait, a hippity hoppity minute... I know that voice.

Trying to remember who it belonged to proved to be a challenge, though. Sorting through my thoughts was about as easy as skipping through a bog.

"Charlee, we've been so worried." Rough fingertips brushed my cheek.

A second voice I recognized came from behind me.

"Sweetheart, you've slept long enough. It's time to wake up."

Wake up? I wasn't a dead smoke show in Hades?

Once more, I tried to open my eyelids or move a finger, to show I was conscious. Despite my best efforts, my brain seemed unable to communicate with my muscles, and I was left exhausted from the effort. Unable to help it, I drifted back into unconsciousness.

THE NEXT TIME I became aware of my surroundings, it was to find someone gently stroking their fingers through my hair. The man sang a haunting melody with heartbreaking lyrics about love and loss. There was an otherworldly beauty to the cadence that reminded me of wolves crying out to the moon.

My body and brain still felt like two separate entities, each refusing to listen to the other, but I desperately wanted to see who was singing to me. I concentrated, focusing all my strength on my eyelids.

Finally, they lifted a tiny crack. But it was enough. Copeland's dark eyes stared back at me.

He was alive. I wanted to shout the words, to tell him I loved him, but my lips refused to obey. Instead, I lay motionless and hoped he wouldn't stop singing.

Copeland must have understood what I wanted because

he began the next verse, all the while his fingers traced the lines of my face. As he got to the chorus once more, a lone wolf's howl joined in. The eerie call blended perfectly with Copeland's voice, as though they'd sung together many times before. The duet sent chills skating over my skin and down my spine.

It took me an embarrassingly long time to realize I was in a hospital and that obnoxious beeping was a heart monitor rather than some type of hellish torture device I'd imagined. But if I was in a hospital, why was a wolf howling in my room? Some hospitals allowed visits from a cat or a dog. I'd even heard of miniature horses visiting hospitals, but I was pretty sure wolves were not on the approved visitors' list.

An arm slid around my waist from behind me. "Welcome back, love," Fletcher murmured, placing a soft kiss at the nape of my neck. "You scared us."

"Hi," I croaked, my lips and mouth dry.

Copeland finished singing and reached for a glass of water on a side table. Sticking his thumb on the end of the straw, he caught some water and held it to my lips. His movements were precise, and he didn't splash so much as a drop on my face. Refusing to let me sit up, he continued until my mouth was no longer as dry as the Sahara Desert.

"Where's Linc? Is he okay?" My vocal cords sounded rusty, making me wonder how long I'd been out.

Copeland uncapped a lip balm and gently ran it across my cracked lips. "Linc's here and he's healed, thanks to you."

There was definitely an implied *but* in there…

"What's wrong?" My stomach clenched, and the tiny sips of water tried to book a round trip out of my stomach.

The heart monitor beeped wildly, summoning a bevy of nurses and doctors to rush toward my room. At least I assumed that's whose footsteps were thundering down the hall. I couldn't be sure; I didn't see their faces since they came to a halt as a vicious snarl echoed through the room.

"Have you been able to get him to shift yet?" a muffled male voice came through the thick wooden door.

"If you come through that door right now, you're signing your own death warrant," Copeland warned.

"We really need to check Charlee's vitals," the man on the other side of the door persisted.

"Believe me, we get that." It was Fletcher who spoke this time. "But Linc isn't in the mood to negotiate or listen to reason."

"Can't you do something?" The guy, who I assumed was a doctor, sounded absolutely exasperated.

"What do you want us to do?" Copeland snapped. "Not even the alpha was able to force him to submit, at least not without risking permanent physical or mental damage."

"What happened?" Tears burned my eyes. Something must have gone wrong and Linc hadn't healed correctly. I'd failed.

"Shh, don't get upset. Linc isn't hurt. And physically, he's fine." Copeland's thumb brushed the tears from my cheek. "But the last thing he remembered before being forcibly held down and sedated was trying to get to you.

When the sedatives wore off and he came to, he was still in protector mode. The staff tried to lock him in a hospital room, but his wolf wasn't having it."

Fletcher snickered. "That's an understatement. I've never seen a piece of wood turned into splinters that fast in my life. If Linc ever gets tired of the mountain hermit thing, he could easily land a commercial role busting through walls to hand out sugary beverages. That door didn't stand a chance."

Copeland rolled his eyes. "Linc chased everyone but Fletcher and me from the room. We're lucky he didn't kill anyone. Now he's refusing to let anyone back inside."

"How long?" I whispered. "How long has he been guarding the room?"

"Three days," Copeland supplied. "We've been giving the medical team updates on your vitals through messages and calls. They aren't happy about it, but they've tolerated it—"

Fletcher snorted. "What choice do they have unless they want to become Linc's chew toy?"

"True," Copeland sighed. "But with Charlee awake, they need to do a thorough examination."

"Linc?" I tried to call his name, but it was little more than a rasp.

Linc must have heard me, because he stopped growling long enough to whine in my direction. I strained, trying to hear if he was coming to me, but heard nothing.

"Take me over to him. I need to see him," I pled. "Please?"

"I don't know." Copeland glanced at the IV lines going into my arm. "You should stay in bed until the doctors have checked you."

"If you don't take them out, I will," I threatened.

"You woke up feisty." Copeland smiled. "But I'm bigger than you, and I think you need to stay in bed."

I narrowed my eyes. "Don't make me get my knife."

"You should probably listen to her, bro." Fletcher yawned and nuzzled the back of my neck. "Charlee's stubborn, and she doesn't make idle threats."

Copeland sighed in defeat. Reluctantly, he pushed himself into a sitting position and began gently unhooking the various wires and tubes.

When he removed the heart monitor, the machine began to blare, making enough racket to wake the dead... which was what the doctors and nurses on the other side of the door must have thought I was because they began pounding harder on the door. One incredibly brave, or stupid, person went so far as to wiggle the door handle.

Linc's already riled-up wolf viewed this as an attack and went into an absolute frenzy. His low warning growls turned to vicious snarls. His jaws snapped angrily as he threw himself at the door.

"She's fine, Linc!" Copeland shouted over the chaos. When the wolf ignored him, he called out to the staff in the hall. "Back away from the door and give us a chance to get the situation under control in here."

The wood of the door creaked and groaned, threatening to give way with each blow from Linc's body. Rather than simply guarding my room, Linc had decided he was going to go to war with anyone he deemed a threat to my safety. It was adorable, especially since I was probably the biggest threat to my safety thanks to my ability to tumble from one mess into another.

Footsteps moved away from the door and back down the hall. Good. Maybe we could get Linc to listen to me with the threat gone.

"I'm going to take you to him, but you better not call him a good boy," Copeland muttered, scooping me out of the bed and into his arms.

"I've heard positive reinforcement training works really well, though!" Fletcher laughed and stretched out on the bed.

"Shut it," Copeland huffed, carrying me toward my frantic wolf mate.

"Just sit me on the floor."

"Yeah, that's not happening," Copeland retorted.

I was about to protest, needing to be eye level with Linc's wolf, but stopped as Copeland lowered himself to sit on the floor instead. He settled me on his lap so that I faced the wolf who was anxiously pacing in front of the door.

"Thank you." I pressed a kiss to his cheek.

His lap was much comfier than the cold linoleum floor of the hospital. And I wasn't about to complain when my body felt as if I'd spent the last few days doing cartwheels to earn a Guinness World Record or something equally ridiculous.

I tried again. "Linc?"

His ears flicked in my direction, but he kept snarling at the door. With his paranormal abilities, he could probably hear every person in the hospital. The wolf's sides heaved, and the fur running from his neck down his spine stood on end.

My heart ached seeing his obvious distress. "Linc, you kept me safe. But I'm awake now, so you don't have to protect me anymore."

The giant wolf turned his head in my direction.

"Come here, love," I said in the universal voice everyone uses when trying to befriend a cute pup.

He whined, but stood his ground, unwilling to leave his post.

I switched tactics, trying to offer him a different job. "Linc, I don't need a protector now. I need you to comfort me."

Holding my breath, I waited to see how he would respond. The wolf's glowing eyes bore into my very soul. Finally, he lifted one gigantic paw and then the other, stalking forward until he stood in front of me.

"Hey there, handsome." I kept my voice soothing, not wanting to startle him.

His imposing size took my breath away. Lowering his head, the wolf pressed his forehead against mine. He sniffed and made a soft chuffing sound.

"He's taking in your scent," Copeland explained, "checking for himself that you're okay."

"Physically or mentally?" I joked, reaching up to rub his fluffy jowls.

"Both," Copeland responded, his tone serious. "Canines are known for their incredible abilities when it comes to tracking scents. Thanks to our supernatural DNA, were-wolves can take it to a whole different level. We can tell roughly how much pain you're in, if you're happy, sad, scared…"

"Wow. That's amazing." I knew Linc had scented my fear in the past, but I didn't realize how much wolf shifters could tell just from a quick sniff.

Copeland continued, "We can also tell if you're sick, although that's not an exact science. For example, we can't tell the exact type of illness, but we can tell if your immune system is struggling with something."

"And you can do this in both forms?" I yelped in surprise as Linc's wet tongue lapped across my face. "Oh, gross! That is not a good boy!"

"Who's the goodest boy now, Linc?" Copeland snickered. "To answer your question, we can smell those things in either form, although things are clearer in our wolf form."

Linc lunged, snapping his teeth inches from Copeland's face, then turned his attention back to me. He pressed his cold nose to my cheek, and then my neck, before lowering his muzzle to poke at my ribs.

"If he wants me to have a full examination, why doesn't he let the doctors in?" My grumble turned to a giggle when he accidentally tickled my ribs.

"Because his wolf nature isn't ready to release control.

He feels better able to control the situation and protect you in this form," Copeland explained.

The door handle wiggled, yanking Linc's attention away from me. He gave a sharp warning bark before trotting over and sniffing under the crack at the bottom of the door. The room rumbled with his angry growls. Linc wasn't hiding his displeasure. He wanted them to know he was still there, and no one was getting into this room until he said so.

"Ignore them. Come back to me," I pled, opening my arms to him.

Linc accepted the invitation and padded back to my side. It amazed me that such a large beast could move without making a sound.

"Remember how I didn't want to shift the day we left the cave? I understand not wanting to shift for fear of being powerless. In my case, I didn't want to shift into my wimpy rabbit form. For you, it's the other way around. While I love both sides of you, right now I really want to feel your arms around me. Please?"

The wolf whined, licking the palm of my hand, still reluctant to obey. But eventually, he dropped to his stomach and let the magic ripple over him, turning his fur back to the bronze tan of his human skin.

"I thought I lost you," were the first words he spoke as he hauled me from Copeland's lap and against his chest, nearly squeezing the air from my lungs.

"But you didn't. Besides, I could say the same. How dare you get sick and scare me like that!" I scowled.

Copeland stood. "Alright. Linc, we need to get her back in bed so the doctors can examine her."

Linc stood, lifting me in his arms as though I weighed nothing more than the ugly blue gown I was wearing. He gently laid me on the bed beside Fletcher, then turned as Copeland said his name.

"And Linc? Put these on. I don't think the staff wants to see your naked butt cheeks."

"I don't really care what the nursing staff wants," Linc scoffed, catching the pair of scrubs mid-air.

The idea of the female nurses seeing him naked sent jealousy sparking through me. "I don't want them seeing you naked."

Linc's head snapped to my face, and his nostrils flared. "You're angry?"

Great, he was back to smelling my emotions again. This was going to take some getting used to.

My cheeks burned. "I just don't like the idea of the nurses seeing you naked. It's irrational, but I can't help it."

"Ah, jealousy. That's a new one." Linc smirked. "And, sugar? I'm happy to dress if it pleases you."

"Well, I wouldn't go that far. If we're being honest, I prefer getting to see you naked," the admission tumbled from my lips before I could stop them. Belatedly, I clamped my hand over my mouth.

"That's also good to know." Linc winked at me.

"For the record, I'd prefer if you stayed completely dressed all the time. Just putting that out there," Fletcher joked.

The men laughed, the last of the tension easing from their tight muscles and fatigue-lined faces. Once he'd slipped on the scrubs, Linc stretched out beside me.

"If you can behave yourself and keep from biting people, I'm going to let the staff in." Copeland directed the comment to Linc, who merely shrugged.

Realizing that was the most assurance he was likely to get, Copeland shook his head and opened the door.

Chapter
TWENTY-FIVE

CHARLEE

Two doctors hurried into the room, followed by half a dozen nurses. Ignoring my protests, they hurried to hook me back up to the various machines.

"When can I go home?" I asked after one doctor finished listening to my heart.

"We're not sure. It could be a while until you're strong enough to be discharged." He patted my arm, then yanked it away when Linc snarled under his breath. "You nearly died, Charlee. Honestly, I'm still not sure how you survived, but I guess sometimes there are miracles that science can't explain. And you're one of them."

When the nurses finished fussing over me, they turned their attention to Fletcher, and for the first time, I noticed there was a bandage wrapped around his arm.

"What happened?" I gasped, scanning his body for other signs of injury.

"Don't look so worried." He caught my chin between his thumb and forefinger. "All I did was give a little blood."

"Your mate gave significantly more than that," the older of the two doctors corrected him. "Every time we tried to stop, he'd demand that we take more. It wasn't until he finally passed out and shut up that we stopped."

My brain was still foggy, and I was struggling to put the pieces together. "Why did you need Fletcher's blood?"

"I wasn't the only one," Fletcher answered before the doctor could. "Monroe and Ellora gave blood as well."

The doctor nodded. "Yes, they did. Using the research you managed to get into our hands, we created a vaccine to give to the wolves prior to exposure. It will save so many lives."

"But why couldn't you use Boone's and my blood?" I didn't like the idea that the others had been put at risk.

"Because we nearly drained you and Boone dry to save Copeland and Linc," the doctor answered. "It will be some time before you're able to give blood again. With the threat of the burrow retaliating with the toxin, Fletcher was unwilling to wait."

I looked at Fletcher, my heart swelling with love and pride that this selfless man was mine. "Thank you." Those two words hardly seemed like enough for everything he'd done for me.

Fletcher guided my face to his and pressed a soft kiss to

my lips. "You have nothing to thank me for. We're family now, which means we're in this together."

"How is Boone?" I asked the doctor after I caught my breath.

"He's doing well. Reese has taken it upon herself to be his caregiver." The doctors exchanged knowing glances, and I caught two of the nurses trying to hide smirks.

"I wouldn't be surprised if he starts asking for more pain meds just to get a break from her." Copeland chuckled. "She can be a bit much."

"She sounds like fun." My memory of meeting Reese was far too fuzzy to make any judgments about her character, but I was looking forward to getting to know her better in the future.

"She seems like trouble," Fletcher corrected.

"Oh, yeah!" Linc laughed and shook his head. "The alpha has wanted to strangle her at least a half dozen times for the escapades and shenanigans she keeps involving Monroe in."

We fell quiet as the doctors took a blood sample, and the nurses finished changing bandages. The doctors promised to check in later. The moment the battered door closed behind them, Linc rolled me to him, his face suddenly stern and unreadable. "I tried to get to you when I found out what you had done."

Avoiding his gaze, I traced his jaw with my fingertips. "I know."

His five o'clock shadow had become a scruffy beard,

giving him sexy lumberjack vibes that I was here for. But it didn't really seem like the best time to tell him that.

"You're angry with me," I observed when he remained silent.

Why wouldn't he be? I'd done the exact opposite of what my mates would have wanted. But I didn't regret it. I knew what I was capable of and had accepted the risks. There was no way I'd apologize for getting the job done. Besides, my apology would be hollow since I'd do the exact same thing if a situation like this arose again.

"No, I'm not angry." Linc caught my fingers between his teeth, gently nipping them.

My eyebrows shot up. "You're not?"

"Of course not," he said as though it was the most logical thing on earth.

Was he purposely messing with my head? How could this man, who seemed to want to control everything, not care that I had gone on such a dangerous jaunt through the burrow?

"No. I'm so dang proud, sugar. You're an incredible woman, and I'm lucky to be your mate." Linc's tongue swirled around my fingers, making it even harder to think clearly.

"I agree." Copeland sat down on the end of the bed and pulled my feet onto his lap. "Although I'm a little annoyed over it."

Fletcher huffed and wrapped an arm around my waist from behind me. "I'm definitely mad about it, but I'm also in awe of our incredible mate."

My heart swelled with happiness. All three of my mates were proud of me.

"Now it's time for you to tell us what happened while you were at Blackberry Burrow." Copeland began massaging my feet.

"Well..." I hesitated, not sure if I should tell them the full truth or not.

"And don't leave out any of the violent parts. Those are my favorite," Linc warned. "Besides, I want to know who did that to your face and bruised your wrist. Because if you didn't kill them, I'm going to."

All three men settled in around me like kids, waiting for a bedtime story. I cleared my throat as a flood of happiness filled my chest. "Well, you see, it's kind of a *bunny* story."

THE MEN HEALED FASTER than me, so they'd been free to come and go while I was stuck inside the four bland white walls. Now that I had my own room, Linc and Copeland had smuggled in a king-size bed while Fletcher caused a distraction in the lab. It took up nearly all the free space, but it was worth it when I got to fall asleep nestled between my mates.

Despite not having to share the room, it still wasn't private. Every time I'd fall asleep, a nurse or doctor would appear to wake me up. I'd been removed from all the machines and I was no longer in danger, but the staff didn't seem to get that memo.

Although, that might have had something to do with the way Monroe and Cillian drilled into their heads that I was to be treated like a princess during my stay. Still, I was grateful for their kindness and friendship. Just that morning, Monroe and Ellora had popped by for a visit.

They shooed the men, as well as the hovering staff, out of my room. Once we were alone, they'd helped me into a bath overflowing with bubbles. While I'd soaked away my stresses, the girls had prepared another surprise for me.

When I'd come out of the bathroom, I'd found pajamas, bras, and panties in every color under the rainbow. Apparently, since my new friends weren't willing to help me escape, they hoped to make the stay more comfortable.

After picking a silky cami and matching pair of booty shorts, I got back under the blanket. Monroe had settled behind me to brush my hair, while Ellora painted my nails. I listened as they shared pack gossip, hardly able to believe this was my life now. By the time they blew me kisses and left, I not only felt human, I felt pretty.

I'd never admit it, but just that little bit of exertion had exhausted me. Scooting down in the bed, I decided to rest my eyes, but that turned into a four-hour nap. I was well-rested and bored out of my mind by the time my guys appeared an hour later.

"Ugh! It's been five days! How much longer are they going to hold me hostage here?" I grumbled as soon as my three mates entered the room.

"Hostage?" Fletcher laughed. "Feeling a bit dramatic, aren't you?"

"If I have to lie here and count the ceiling panels one more time, I swear I'm going to die of boredom," I grumbled. "You guys get to come and go, but when I tried to sneak to the vending machine for a candy bar, I was tackled and hauled back to this room. One nurse threatened to handcuff me to the bed!"

"Did she happen to leave the handcuffs?" Copeland asked, wiggling his eyebrows.

"Unfortunately, no," I huffed. "Practicing how to escape them would have given me something to do."

"I have an idea." Copeland pulled his phone from his pocket and tapped the screen a few times before handing it to me. "That's my Kindle account. My credit card is linked, so buy whatever books interest you. Go crazy."

"Ooh!" I barely kept myself from snatching his phone from his hand.

Lost in the whole new world that had just been opened to me, I didn't notice the guys moving around the room or the nurses coming in to check on me.

"That was a serious error in judgment on your part, Copeland. With so many books at her fingertips, I think she's forgotten we exist." Fletcher sat down on the bed beside me, but I still didn't look up. "She's probably already fallen for a half dozen book boyfriends."

"Maybe she needs to be reminded why real boyfriends are better." The foot of the bed sank as Linc leaned over to rest his palms on it.

I didn't look up. "Shh. I just got to the good part."

"Is that so?" Fletcher asked, amusement thick in his tone.

"The good part?" Linc growled, the bed sinking more as his full weight settled on it.

Biting my newly painted nail, I didn't bother to answer them as I tapped to turn the page.

It wasn't until lips brushed my ankle and moved up the inside of my leg that I looked up. "What are you... ooh!"

Linc was lying between my legs, covered by the blanket, and his mouth was making its way up my inner thigh. Gripping my hips, he gently pulled me so that my back no longer rested on the headboard, but was now flat on the mattress.

"I think we can help ease your boredom." Fletcher lifted the blanket and climbed into the bed, stretching out on my right side while Copeland mirrored him on my left.

"You guys don't get it. Just give me five more minutes and I'll put it down!" My eyes darted back to the phone in my hand. "It's a forced-proximity romance, and things are getting steamy..."

Linc's thumbs hooked around the band of my booty shorts and slid them down. Without any warning, his tongue traced my slit.

"What are you reading that has you so wet, sugar?" Copeland's hand curled around mine, turning the phone so he could see the screen. To my absolute horror, he began to read out loud.

"Pick up your fork, Ari. The detective is going to get suspicious.
Rez's voice was liquid honey in my mind, each word an intimate stroke. His fingers flicked across my G-spot, and I saw stars.

I picked up my fork, each movement mechanical as I fought to control my facial expressions and my body's response to the touch of my mates. Giving Jack a smile, I put another bite of pasta in my mouth, this one much smaller. The last thing I wanted was someone yanking me out of my chair to give me the Heimlich maneuver because I'd choked.

Zon's finger slid inside me, and my soul tried to leave the chat. I wanted to cry. Maybe beg them to stop, or beg them for more."

Fletcher's hand slipped beneath my cami. "I had no idea you were into naughty books, Charlee." His fingers brushed against my breast, causing my body to flush.

Linc's lips pressed against my slick entrance, not moving, just letting the heat of his mouth drive me crazy.

Copeland leaned toward me, capturing my lips in a painfully delicious kiss. Pulling away, he tapped the screen and continued reading, although I was struggling to make sense of the words.

"Focus on my voice, Zon ordered.

My body obeyed instantly.

Good girl. I grew wetter at Zon's praise. His finger danced with Rez's as they pumped and stroked…"

Copeland stopped reading as my back arched off the bed. Linc had chosen that moment to press his tongue inside me.

"Linc! We can't! Not here!" I tried to pull my legs together.

He ignored me, prying my legs apart and opening me to him. Fletcher licked and kissed his way up my neck, while his thumb brushed my nipple.

Copeland cleared his throat and began to read again, his voice thick with desire.

"You like that Jack is across the table and could catch on at any minute. Don't you, baby?

My walls tightened around their fingers.

I felt that. Such a naughty girl, Zon growled in my mind.

What was wrong with me? I'd never taken risks like this before. If Jack caught us, I would be humiliated.

Would you? Or would you like it if I offered him a taste of your cream? Zon asked, voice rough.

My body trembled.

That's what I thought. I glanced at Zon as he spoke in my mind, but he seemed to be ignoring me. He was relaxed, taking his time with the last of the food on his plate.

Taking a quick peek at Rez, I watched in disbelief as he talked to Jack about a burglary he'd seen on the news that morning. Neither man gave away even a hint that they had their fingers buried inside me. The risk and the naughtiness had lust tearing at my insides. I fought to keep my breathing even, but the effort was making me lightheaded. I needed release.

When I tell you to, you're going to come..."

"Copeland! Please stop!" I begged.

All three men paused what they were doing, and Fletcher pushed himself up onto his elbow to peer down at me. "Do you really want to stop, Charlee?"

I started to answer, but Linc cut me off, his voice muffled beneath the blanket. "And don't lie. The taste of your desire is on my tongue and the scent of your need is heavy in the air."

"It doesn't matter what I want; we have to stop. A nurse could walk in any minute!" My heart pounded. "How would we explain what's going on? 'Oh, Fletcher's checking the pulse in my neck, Copeland's testing my reflexes, and Linc is doing mouth-to-muff resuscitation! Nothing to see here!'"

My mates lost it, howling with laughter.

"I'm glad you think it's funny," I huffed. "You guys don't know how annoying it is to be interrupted in the middle of a book, and how frustrating it is to have three sexy mates at my disposal but having to resist."

"Who says you have to resist?" Copeland purred, dropping his head and sucking my left nipple into his mouth through my silky shirt.

"Yeah, from what Copeland just read, I think you might like the idea that someone could walk in and see us worshiping your body." Fletcher cupped my right breast and placed soft kisses along my jaw. "Does that excite you?"

"No," I lied. "Well, I don't know. It's not like I've been in this situation before."

Linc began to lap along my slit, each stroke of his tongue hard and slow. I opened my mouth to protest, but it turned to a gasp as he focused his attention on my clit and slipped a finger inside me. With the three men touching, teasing, and turning me on, I didn't stand a chance.

When Linc's finger disappeared, a pathetic whimper escaped my throat. His tongue quickly filled me. This time, it felt different. Was it possible for it to be longer and rougher? Who cared what was possible when it felt so incredible having it licking so deep inside me?

"Linc." His name came out as a moan. Reaching beneath the blanket, I sank my fingers into his hair. "Don't stop. Please."

He pressed harder, adding friction and sending me over the edge.

My lips parted, but before I could make a sound, Fletcher caught my mouth and devoured my cry. The mattress shifted as Linc's mouth disappeared from between my thighs.

"Is everything okay in here?"

I jerked in shock. Why hadn't I heard the door open?

"We're fine, but Charlee is feeling exhausted after having company today. She'd like to be left alone for the rest of the evening. We're all staying, so if there is a problem, we'll let you know." Copeland's voice was polite and professional.

His broad shoulders blocked her from seeing me, but I still didn't understand how he could sound so unfazed while his fingers slipped between my thighs, stroking me toward a second climax before I'd even caught my breath from the first.

"You can also click the call button on the wall behind—"

"Out," Linc snapped, slightly harsher than necessary.

"Yes, sir!" The door shut with a soft click.

I peeked over Copeland's shoulder, watching Linc stride across the floor and lock the door.

"Do you think she knew what you were doing to me?" How was I going to be able to look the nurse in the face the next time she checked on me?

"Stop panicking, sugar. I was by the window before the door opened," Linc assured me. A sly grin slid across his face. "I heard her coming before you started coming."

My face burned, and I dropped back on the pillow with a groan. "I'm just going to go back into a coma and stay there until she retires."

"Oh no you're not." Fletcher rolled me toward him. "You told us you're bored, and we're here to entertain you."

He ran his hand through my hair to the back of my head. Pulling me close, he captured my mouth.

Copeland's lips brushed my neck, and his hand trailed down my back and over my hip. "Little rabbit, you need to trust us to protect you. The nurse didn't see anything, so stop overthinking it."

Linc leaned against the windowsill behind Fletcher. "If she's able to think, you two aren't doing your job."

Fletcher pulled my leg over his hip as he licked his way down my throat. Copeland cradled my breast, his thumb flicking over my nipple.

"Oh!" I gasped, my body responding to their every touch.

"That's better," Linc praised.

I glanced at him over Fletcher's shoulder and licked my lips as I caught sight of the tent in his pants. There was no denying the man was built to please. Linc realized what I was looking at and, rather than shifting positions to hide it, he unbuttoned his jeans. He let them slip down just enough to free his erection.

Linc's eyes locked with mine. "Tell us what you want."

I hesitated.

"You had no problem giving orders while you were waving a knife around in the burrow. Would it help if I got you another blade?" Copeland shifted his hips, pressing his hardened length against my butt.

Fletcher hissed as the move caused me to grind against him. "Tell us what you want." His fingers tightened in my hair.

Channeling the confident woman I'd been on my mission, I met Linc's challenging gaze. "I want to watch you stroke yourself while Fletcher fills me."

Without taking his glowing eyes from mine, Linc gripped his cock and ran his hand slowly up its length, veins bulging... and I didn't just mean in his arm.

"Fletcher," I rasped his name, squirming against him. "Hurry!"

The rabbit shifter slid a hand between our bodies, unbuttoning his pants. His erection sprung free with the eager energy of the Easter Bunny on Easter morning.

Fletcher lined himself up with my entrance, guiding himself inside me one slow inch at a time. Blinking hard, I tried to uncross my eyes so I could watch Linc.

My blood flushed with heat, then chills, as pleasure and lust shot through my body. I reached behind me, fumbling with Copeland's pants. Saying nothing about my clumsy attempts, Copeland shoved his jeans over his hips. I found the prize I was seeking.

Wrapping my fingers around him, I stroked, enjoying the feel of the silken steel against my skin. Copeland groaned, his hips jerking forward.

Fletcher rested his palm on my butt, tucking me against him as his hips found a steady rhythm. My hand kept pace as it moved along Copeland's length. Linc matched us as he continued to stroke his cock. We were in perfect sync, and I loved it.

Our breathing grew ragged, and Fletcher's fingers dug into my skin. "I can't hold out much longer, love."

"Then don't," I gasped.

That was all he needed to pick up the pace. He rocked faster, burying himself deeper with each thrust. The need for release grew heavy in my belly. When his hips shifted slightly and he stroked my G-spot just right, my orgasm exploded without warning.

I tried to scream his name, but no sound came out, and my eyes rolled so far, I thought I could see the back of my brain. My body clamped around Fletcher, milking him as pulses of pleasure traveled through me.

"Charlee." Fletcher buried his face in my hair and groaned my name. "You feel so good, love."

Lost in my explosive climax, I forgot I held Copeland's erection in my tightly clenched hand, until he roared my name and I felt his release splash my skin.

Panting and greedy, I watched as Linc's muscles strained and his cock jerked in his grip. He never broke eye contact as he joined us in riding the aftershocks of our orgasms. The man was completely unembarrassed as he let me soak in the sight of him.

I'd never felt so powerful or desired as I did in that moment, basking in the love of my mates.

Chapter TWENTY-SIX

CHARLEE

"If you start feeling overwhelmed or tired, tell us, okay?" Copeland wrapped a blanket around my legs. "I don't care if the alpha requested your presence. We'll get you out of there immediately."

"Would you stop fussing?" Laughing, I batted his hand away. "I'm a big girl and can handle myself. Which reminds me, is this wheelchair really necessary? My legs still work."

"You've been in a hospital room for over a week. We're not going to risk exhausting you the first day Dr. Blaine is allowing you out of here," Fletcher explained.

"I don't like it when the three of you gang up on me. You guys get so bossy," I playfully huffed.

"If you prefer, I'll be happy to carry you," Linc offered.

My cheeks warmed. It was embarrassing enough that I was going to be wheeled in front of the alpha. But to be carried in front of him? With our size difference, it would look like Linc was carrying a kid instead of his bonded mate.

"Um… I think I'll stick with the wheelchair."

"Suit yourself," Linc shrugged. "Just let me know if you change your mind."

"Do we know why the alpha wants to see me?" I asked, fiddling with the fringe on the edge of the pastel plaid blanket.

"It's a surprise," Copeland whispered in my ear before standing and pushing the wheelchair down the hallway.

A sleek, cobalt blue SUV was waiting at the curb in front of the hospital. The moment we stepped outside, the driver hopped out and hurried around to open the side doors of the vehicle.

"Your ride awaits, milady." The sweet, older gentleman gave me a wink, and his bushy mustache turned up in a smile.

"How nice!" I beamed back at him. "Thank you, kind sir."

He tipped an imaginary cap and waited until we'd all slid into the back seat before shutting the door and making his way back around to the driver's seat.

"Do you know where we're going?" I asked, resting my head on Fletcher's shoulder and lacing my fingers through Copeland's.

"You'll see." Copeland gave my hand a squeeze. "Be patient, little rabbit."

We'd driven for about an hour when things began to look familiar.

Surely we aren't going there...

I kept the thought to myself, unable to believe what my eyes were telling me. But as the miles passed, it became clear that we were headed back to the last place on earth I ever wanted to visit. Blackberry Burrows.

"Tell him to stop," I squeaked, hardly able to speak through the tightness in my throat. My pulse pounded in my ears. "Please!"

Fletcher turned, catching my chin and forcing me to meet his gaze. "Breathe, Charlee. You're safe. No one is going to touch you."

"You can't be serious!" I half-shrieked, half-sobbed. "My last visit there didn't exactly earn me any friends."

"I think you're going to find you have a lot more friends than you realize once we get there," Fletcher tried to reassure me.

"And I think you've lost your mind." I hadn't meant to say it, but I couldn't help it.

Had he forgotten what I'd done to obtain the information about the toxin? It had involved threats, a knife, and a whole roll of duct tape. There wasn't a chance in Hades the burrow or the council was going to welcome me back with open arms.

"The alpha is already there with some of the pack. And they're waiting on you." Linc's calm tone quieted my rising panic. "We don't want to ruin the surprise, but let's just say the council is no longer calling the shots."

"Oh." Not sure what else to say, I slumped back against the car seat and remained quiet.

What could've gone down in the past week to make my mates feel so confident it was safe for me to return to the burrow?

"Right on time," the driver declared, rolling through the open gates of Blackberry Burrow.

Sitting up tall, I peered out the windshield, and my jaw dropped.

At least half of the pack was filling the courtyard in front of us. Alpha Cillian, Cyrus, Rig, and Monroe stood in front of them. Monroe radiated pure excitement as she bounced on the balls of her feet.

But the biggest shock of all, and what had me gripping the edge of the seat, was seeing the entire council on their knees on the sidewalk. Their wrists and ankles were shackled, and a chain linked the men together. Pack security stood behind them, guarding them closely.

The SUV rolled to a stop, and Copeland reached for the door handle. "I'll get your wheelchair. Hold on just a moment."

"No." I grabbed his sleeve. "I don't want it. Please."

His brows drew together, and it was clear he was about to disagree, but something in my expression stopped him.

"I promise you can smother me all you want once we leave and I'll love every minute of it! But after everything they put me through, I want to stand tall and look down on them." It was spiteful and a little mean. But let's be real, they deserved it and more.

"Dang, girl! You're hot when you're vengeful." Linc

rumbled in approval, sending me a look that had my stomach performing a perfect gymnastic floor routine.

"Well then, lead the way." Copeland sat back in his seat and motioned for me to step out first. "We'll follow you... our wee warrior."

It was a shame I'd worked so hard to save him, only to have to kill him a week later.

He'd picked the perfect moment to use the nickname, since I couldn't make a scene with everyone watching. Fletcher and Linc dissolved into laughter.

Copeland's cocky grin told me he thought he'd won, and that wasn't going to fly. Making my way over his lap to exit the car, I 'accidentally' planted a foot between his legs. Hard. His wince told me I'd hit my mark.

"You better watch yourself before I ask the alpha for an extra set of those chains," I warned.

Copeland wiggled his eyebrows and swatted my butt. "Don't tempt me with a good time."

"I swear I don't know what I'm going to do with you!" I mumbled under my breath, exiting the car with as much grace as I could muster.

Without a word, the men filed out and moved to stand at my back. They were a wall of power ready to take down anyone who dared to touch me. Some of my stress melted away.

This was so much better than sneaking in under the cover of darkness with nothing but a knife, and I wasn't ashamed to admit it. There was nothing wrong with being strong, nor was there any shame in being protected.

"You're finally here!" Monroe squealed, running up and throwing her arms around my neck.

"She's perfectly on time," Alpha Cillian commented from behind her.

"Yeah, well, it felt like we had to wait forever to show her our surprise!" Monroe protested.

Alpha Cillian held out his hand for me to shake. "Charlee, we want to thank you for the great service you did not only for our pack, but for all the wolf packs around the US."

I couldn't have hidden my confusion if I'd wanted to. "But I'm the one who brought the trouble to your doorstep."

"No, you were the catalyst that brought the potential threat to our attention. And then you risked everything in order to right the wrongs that had been done—wrongs that you had no part in creating. Our pack wanted to honor your bravery and sacrifice by rectifying the wrongs that were done to you." The alpha motioned toward the people in chains.

My eyes trailed over the faces of the men, and a couple of women, who were bound in chains. Each of them had taken part in my years of torture and mistreatment. They'd either ordered it, or they'd done it at their own hand. Not a single face was missing.

"How did you know?" I asked.

Was it possible the wolves were mind readers? Had they forced the council to confess to how they'd treated me?

Copeland rested a hand on my shoulder. "While we

took turns staying with you at the hospital, Fletcher helped us gain access to all the records that we needed. It turns out the council keeps very detailed files on every female rabbit in Blackberry Burrow."

I twisted my head to look up at Fletcher, surprised to find his eyes shimmering with unshed tears. "Why didn't you tell me, Charlee? I didn't know it was that bad."

He'd been there to witness the big things like when I'd been tossed in front of the council, and when they'd ordered that I be imprisoned, caged, or beaten. But there was more he'd known nothing about. All the small punishments, the insults, the deprivation, and the cruelties done behind closed doors.

"If you had known, you would have done something stupid. Something that probably would've gotten you killed. Just because my life was in ruins didn't mean yours had to be as well," I answered honestly. "Fletcher, I've loved you for as long as I can remember, and seeing you happy was the only thing that brought me joy. Besides, I didn't want to waste the precious minutes we were able to steal away by pouring out my burdens. I wanted to pretend those things didn't exist and focus on our time together."

Fletcher pulled me into a hug, nearly crushing me.

"I need to breathe," I wheezed when he didn't let go.

The alpha cleared his throat. "Once Fletcher located the records, your mates hunted down every single person mentioned. While they did that, the rest of the pack scoured the rest of the records to get an idea of exactly what we were dealing with and how to fix things. Unfortunately, there wasn't a single person on the council with clean hands. None of them deserve to be in any position of power, so it's time for change at Blackberry Burrow."

"I couldn't agree more. But how is that going to work? Most, if not all, of the male rabbits like the way the council runs things. If they are allowed to vote in the burrow leaders, they'll pay lip service to what the alpha demands while continuing to do the same things behind the scenes." As much as I wanted to be hopeful, I had my doubts that change was possible.

Monroe hopped in before the alpha could continue. "That's why we've asked you to come here. And feel free to say no!" She reached out and squeezed my hand. "Trust me, I know all about the nightmares a place from our past can hold. And if you decide you never want to step foot in Blackberry Burrow again after today, we will back you 100%."

The alpha nodded. "The decision is yours. But we'd like for you, and your mates, to consider taking over Blackberry Burrow. If you didn't want to stay permanently, it could be a temporary arrangement."

My jaw hit the sidewalk. "You can't be serious."

"Dead serious," the alpha confirmed.

"But how would we...?" I trailed off, my eyes scanning the place that had once been my home and my prison.

Women and children lined the streets on either side, their gazes nervously darting from the wolves scattered around, to the council, then to me. It was what I saw in their gazes, something I'd never seen before, that stopped me from turning the alpha down and making a beeline for the SUV.

Hope.

They wanted things to change, and this was probably their only shot at making that happen.

"There's so much to be done." My legs wobbled as I thought about the amount of work we were facing.

"Which is why you wouldn't be doing it alone. We've made some preliminary plans to help streamline the process for you." Cillian motioned around the grounds. "The women have been moved from the dorm building, and now the males are living there. The prison is under the control of my most trusted security team. They'll bring the prisoners out daily, and have them work in the burrow while staying under close guard. All the men who don't have productive jobs will join that workforce."

Monroe squeezed my hand, barely containing her excitement. "They'll be working to build houses so each woman will have a house to share with her children. Boone and Reese are willing to stay as well. Boone is eager to revamp the entire lab in order to create a steady supply of the vaccine that can be distributed to packs around the US, as well as continue researching an antidote."

"Wow." There was so much I wanted to say, but words escaped me.

Linc laughed. "I'm pretty sure Reese is just hoping for a chance to knock some heads together."

Monroe rolled her eyes. "You're not wrong. But she could be a positive influence on the women. Not to mention, she would be great at monitoring the interactions between the male rabbits and the females to make sure no manipulation is happening."

"It's possible there are couples, or fluffles, that would love the chance to be together." Her brow creased with worry. "But I think the females are going to need to learn how to set boundaries first. They need to see that a different way of life is possible, and feel safe while they get used to it."

"Exactly," Alpha Cillian agreed. "That's why we want Reese and Boone, as well as some of our pack, to stay here at Blackberry Burrow. They will help with security, but also with anything else you need to create a beautiful haven."

"It's something I would have loved the chance to do to my own burrow," Monroe added, her tone wistful.

Cillian noticed, and his stern expression softened. "And you will soon," he promised, brushing his knuckles against her cheek. "Now that we know other burrows were involved in the capture and death of wolf shifters, as well as working to create a distribution network for the toxin, many of the burrows are going to find themselves under new management. This isn't a problem with a single burrow, and it's past time they were stopped."

"Ellora wanted to be here, but she's already on the way to her burrow with her mates at her side," Monroe told me, her eyes sparkling with excitement. "While going through Blackberry Burrow's records, it was discovered that they'd placed a large order for the toxin. And since a weapon like that breaks paranormal law, they're overturning the leadership there as well. It's time for change."

I couldn't agree more. For years, I'd dreamed about a life outside of the burrow. A life where I'd be loved and protected. It had never occurred to me that it might be possible to have those things here.

"What do you guys think?" I asked, searching my mates' faces. "Are you really willing to leave the mountain? I know you love it."

"Sugar," Linc said, giving me a slow, lazy smile, "I'll follow you to the ends of the earth as long as I get to hold you in my arms at night."

"And you?" I asked, looking up at Copeland.

"We locked ourselves away, hurt from past attempts at failing to find a mate. It's time for us to leave our self-imposed isolation and experience new adventures with you"—Copeland exchanged glances with Linc and Fletcher —"with *our family*. This seems like a pretty good place to start."

It wasn't going to be easy, but nothing worth fighting for ever was. I would make Blackberry Burrow a wonderful place to live. And I'd enjoy knowing that the men who'd once made me feel so small would be forced to watch me undo every indignity they'd forced upon those weaker than them.

Oh, yeah. I was definitely going to enjoy this.

ABOUT SEDONA ASHE

Sedona Ashe doesn't reserve her sarcasm for her books; her poor husband can tell you that her wit, humor, and snarky attitude are just part of her daily life. While she loves writing paranormal shifter reverse harem novels, she's a sucker for true love, twisted situations, and wacky humor.

Sedona lives in a small town at the base of the Great Smoky Mountains in Tennessee. She and her husband share their home with their three children, adorable pup, five cats, two pet foxes, chickens, three crazy turkeys, two cows, and over a hundred reptiles.

When she isn't working, she enjoys getting away from the computer to hike, free dive, travel, study languages, and capture the essence of places and people in her photography. She has a crazy goal of writing one million words in a year and spending six months exploring Indonesia.